HIT AND MISFIRE

Slocum shoved Porges to one side, raised the soaking wet derringer, and fired at the dark figure racing at them from across the street. The small gun made a popping sound unlike the sharp snap Slocum was used to. But the round flew straight and true, for the attacker skidded to a halt and turned away as if injured. It took Slocum a second to realize that the sound had come from the *other* man's gun. The derringer had misfired! Slocum cocked the pistol and fired again.

Nothing but a dull click. The dark figure ran away silently. Twice Slocum had fired, twice the weapon had failed him.

"I don't know why he left. That was a five-shot pistol he had and he saw the derringer . . ." Slocum stopped and stared. Michael Porges lay on the hard cobblestones, clutching his bleeding belly.

The single shot had found its target, and their assailant had run off because he had succeeded in his deadly mission.

JAKE LOGAN

SLOCUM AND THE RICH MAN'S SON

JOVE BOOKS, NEW YORK

This is a work of fiction. Names, characters, places and incidents are either the product of the author's imagination or are used fictitiously, and any resemblance to actual persons, living or dead, business establishments, events or locales is entirely coincidental.

SLOCUM AND THE RICH MAN'S SON

A Jove Book / published by arrangement with the author

PRINTING HISTORY
Jove edition / March 2001

The Penguin Putnam Inc. World Wide Web site address is
http://www.penguinputnam.com

ISBN: 0-515-13029-X

A JOVE BOOK®
Jove Books are published by The Berkley Publishing Group,
a division of Penguin Putnam Inc.
375 Hudson Street, New York, New York 10014.
JOVE and the "J" design
are trademarks belonging to Penguin Putnam Inc.

PRINTED IN THE UNITED STATES OF AMERICA

10 9 8 7 6 5 4 3 2 1

1

John Slocum did not know whether to rest his hand on the ebony butt of his Colt Navy in its cross-draw holster or to grab his poke. He had almost three hundred dollars riding high in his shirt pocket. And the Sydney Duck Saloon was not the kind of dive to reveal any money, much less a wad big enough to choke a cow. The saloon at the foot of Clark's Wharf was filled with sailors from all over the world, swearing and shouting in a half dozen different languages. In the dark distance, Slocum heard the faint chiming of a buoy warning merchant ships coming into San Francisco Bay of the shallow spots to avoid.

He wished he didn't have to be going from one deadfall and bagnio and saloon to another hunting for a rich man's son, but he had taken Nathan Porges's money and was not going to quit now. A growing sense that Michael Porges was in big trouble drove him now, all the more that he had finally gotten a whiff of the trail after hunting through the lowest of the low dives in San Francisco. Slocum forced himself into a small cranny at the far end of the stained, broken bar and dropped a silver dollar for a shot of watered whiskey. Even through the smoke and din of the saloon, the barkeep heard the silvery ring on the bar and came to deliver a shot of questionable whiskey.

Slocum sniffed cautiously, wondering if it might be laced with a Mickey Finn. Barkeeps in this part of San Francisco were notorious for working with shanghaiers. Give an unwary reveler a knockout drink loaded with chloral hydrate and he woke up miles at sea on a China Clipper heading for the Celestial Kingdom. Sipping, Slocum decided the drink was not doctored. It tasted too much like water for that. The more potent the drink poured in a cheap saloon like the Sydney Duck, the warier he had to be that he drank more than whiskey.

For two days Slocum had hunted Michael Porges. Every step of the way convinced him the scion of the railroad tycoon did not want to be found by anyone, much less his father. The elder Porges was certain his son had been kidnapped, but Slocum quickly found that Michael wanted only to go on a bender. Somewhere along the way, Michael had learned of Slocum and had made every effort possible to fade into the rich tapestry of people flowing along the San Francisco waterfront.

"You lookin' for some fun, mister? I ain't seen one like you in here in a long time. Maybe never."

Slocum started to tell the whore to leave him be, but something about her caught his attention. For all her threadbare dress and outright filth, there was something different, even elegant, about her. The contrast in the way she looked and Slocum's first impression made her a curiosity. In a place like the Sydney Duck Saloon that meant something.

That meant danger.

"I'm Florrie. What's your name? Oh, never mind. You'd only tell me a lie just like the rest of 'em." Florrie sidled closer and put a hand on his shoulder. "A man so big and strong can tell me any lie he wants, I reckon."

Florrie's clothing had been fine—once. It now hung in

tatters, revealing enticing portions of bare flesh beneath. Again Slocum was caught in the contradictions. Her hands were filthy and her nails caked with grime, but the skin showing under the ragged clothing seemed well scrubbed and lacking in the sores and insect bites sported by most soiled doves on the waterfront. She was of average height and had her fire-red hair pulled back severely in a snood. He tried to make out her face, but she stood in shadows, angling her face to keep from being seen clearly. What he could see of her, it appeared as if the dirt on her face had been applied as carefully as makeup.

"Why do you think I'd lie?" he asked.

"All men lie," she said with unfeigned bitterness. Slocum recoiled a little. Such anger ran deep and might carry a sudden knife with it.

"You fallen on hard times?" he asked. The Panic of '73 had brought ruin to many businesses throughout the West. Florrie might have lost a husband and a fortune and ended up doing the only thing she could to stay alive.

She might have, but that seemed wrong to Slocum. This kept him from chasing her away, although the flash of pure hatred across her face should have been a warning. Her brown eyes swirled with flecks of gold, and she looked harder—and softer—than a demimonde ought to.

"Ain't none of your business if I have," she said, tossing her head and holding her chin up high. Then she smiled crookedly and said, "It's my business to give *you* a hard time." She grabbed for his crotch, but he was faster. He caught her wrist and held it firmly. Whatever else Florrie was, she was strong. Slocum had to strain just a bit more than he had thought likely as she twisted in his grip.

"Well, Mr. High and Mighty. You think *you're* the one sellin' it?" she said haughtily.

"I'm paying," Slocum said cautiously. "For the right information."

"I ain't no snitcher."

"I'm not the law," Slocum said. "I'm not a Special, either. Nobody's hired me to keep this place decent." He looked around the Sydney Duck and knew the saloon would have to be burned to the ground and then plowed under for that. Two men robbed a drunk in a far corner. Another Cyprian had found her a seafaring john and the two of them made love on a rickety table in another corner. A small crowd gathered around them, placing wagers on both the sailor's and the hooker's performances.

"There's nothin' I know that you'd want to know. But I can *show* you a thing or two. A dollar. And I won't cheat you. You'll get your money's worth, I promise." Florrie moved closer again. This time Slocum let her. For all the dirt on her face and hands, she didn't reek, showing, she had bathed recently. Maybe within the week.

"I'm looking for a man," Slocum said. He felt the pressure of time on him now. The more he sought Michael Porges, the more he felt the young man was going to run headlong into trouble he couldn't handle. Slocum had lived by his wits and his instincts all his life. His gut told him he had better find Porges fast or he'd have to tell Nathan Porges he had a son to bury.

"And I've found me one," Florrie said.

Slocum looked over her shoulder and saw two sailors coming in his direction. They poked and nudged one another as they summoned courage to take Florrie away from him. The trail had led Slocum here, and a twisted one it had been. Porges had been living closer and closer to the edge as he gambled, drank, and smoked tins of opium bought along Dupont Gai in Chinatown. Slocum dared not get in a fight that would delay him now, especially over a whore.

"His name is Porges, Michael Porges," Slocum said. He felt the woman stiffen. Florrie took a step back so she could fix a steely look on him.

"What do you want with him?"

"That's my business, but I mean him no harm. You do know him, don't you?"

Slocum saw the woman turn cagey.

"Maybe I do, maybe I don't."

"Two dollars," Slocum said. He could afford it. The elder Porges had been generous in payment. That lump of greenbacks worried Slocum as the sailors came closer. He sensed that Florrie was not simply toying with him and that the woman knew Porges' whereabouts.

"Ten!"

"Done," he said, not wanting to argue with her. "Where can we go to talk about it? You have a crib nearby?"

"I got me a room," Florrie said proudly, locking her arm through his and leading him across the room, twisting and turning agilely to avoid contact with the saloon patrons, flaunting her charms and openly displaying her conquest to the other soiled doves. Slocum heaved a sigh of relief when they left behind the sailors who had been homing in on them. The salts had been drunk and looked like mean customers hankering for a fight.

He would have hated to kill them. But he would have if it meant staying on Michael's trail. Slocum had taken Nathan Porges's commission because he needed the money but had come to realize how desperate the man's son was and how self-destructive he might be. Usually, Slocum would not have cared, but this time he did. In Michael Porges he saw too much of himself a few years earlier.

He had been uppity and sure of himself, and his arrogance in the face of soulless men like William Quantrill and Bloody Bill Anderson had left him gut-shot and dying. Only his anger at the cowardly deed and his own steel will had kept him alive. Wounded but healing, he had returned to Slocum's Stand in Calhoun, Georgia, only to find a carpetbagger judge and a hired gunman wanting land that had been in his family since King George II had

deeded it to his great-grandfather. Slocum had stood up
for his rights and had been dodging the wanted posters
for judge killing ever since. In Michael Porges he saw the
potential for the same kind of wildness, the same determination—and the same dangerous road being taken.

"We got to talk right away?" The woman moved closer.
Slocum pushed Florrie away, even as he felt himself responding to her nearness. He had to keep his mind on the
search for Michael Porges. The young man's life might
depend on how fast he could be found.

"What do you know about Porges?" Slocum asked.

"Not out here. In my room," Florrie said, looking
around. They left the Sydney Duck Saloon and walked a
half block toward the Embarcadero. The stench of rotting
fish put Slocum on edge as much as the danger he courted
in the person of Florrie. He followed her up rickety steps
to a second floor. From a few rooms came the sounds of
passion. Slocum tried to keep his attention on Florrie, but
this worked against him, too. She wiggled her behind in
just the right way to excite him.

"Come on in, big boy," she said, opening the door to
a tiny room hardly large enough to hold the shabby mattress on the floor. She made him force his way past her.
He sucked in his breath as he felt her breasts rubbing
against his body. Slocum swung around and faced her,
not willing to put up with any more dilly-dallying.

"Where's—" Slocum began. He found himself with an
armful of willing, wanton woman. Florrie kissed him hard
on the lips and ground her body into his. Her legs parted
slightly so she could capture his thigh between her upper
legs. She began rubbing herself against his leg. He felt
her excitement, and it communicated to him. Florrie was
a good-looking woman under all that dirt. Good-looking
and intoxicating. It had, been too long since he'd had a
woman, any woman.

"No," he protested—to no avail. Florrie was not to be

denied now that she had him alone in her room.

"I want you. You excite me more than any of those sailors. You're a real man. I *know* it!" Her body kept moving sinuously against his, insistently demanding more from him. Then her hand closed on his crotch.

"I have to know about Porges. You know anything or not?"

"The only way I'll tell you is . . . after," she said.

Slocum pushed back from her, staring down into her feverish eyes. They carried a hint of madness now.

"How do I know you have anything to say?"

"Keep the money," she said in a husky whisper. Her hands moved restlessly over his body, his chest, lower. "Keep it, make love to me, and I'll tell you where Michael went."

"Michael," Slocum repeated. "Tell me something about him."

The woman started to protest, then the madness faded for a moment. She took a deep breath that caused her breasts to rise and then fall heavily, momentarily distracting Slocum. He was all too aware of her charms and his attraction to them.

"He has a scar," she said. "Here." She made a long slash across her belly. "He is running from a man named Simpson over a gambling debt. Michael has a habit of drawing to inside straights when he gambles."

This startled Slocum. He had discovered this only after talking with more than one tinhorn gambler in the past couple days. It was hardly the sort of thing a man buying a woman's favors would mention. Florrie could have found out about the scar—Slocum had no idea if Michael Porges had one in the place she said—but he could not see how she would learn of his gambling flaws.

"His middle name's Godfrey," she said in a low voice. Then Florrie looked up at Slocum and the wildfire returned to her eyes. She seemed to grow, to change, to become someone else, someone with a passion too great to be contained by her body.

Slocum remembered Michael's father showing him a picture with the young man's full name written on the back. Slocum wondered how Florrie could have found out such diverse things about the young Porges. However she had done it, he had no doubt she knew Michael.

Florrie became more insistent, her kisses hard and her teeth nipping just a little bit at his lower lip. The woman moved the center of her oral attentions when he started to protest. She kissed Slocum's ear and then thrust her tongue into it as she whispered, "I want something hard in me. You look like you're a real stallion. Let's see!"

Slocum let her unfasten his gun belt. He kicked it out of the way as she unbuttoned his fly. Then he stopped trying to stop her from doing things to him and started enjoying them. Florrie's lips closed on the tip of his raging manhood, then her mouth engulfed him entirely. Slocum felt his legs turning to water. He sank down slowly, the woman following his every movement. She gobbled and licked and used her mouth on his organ until Slocum was afraid he would get off like a young buck getting his first piece of tail.

"No, no more," he said. "You're too good." Florrie looked up at him, a wicked grin on her lips and her eyes even madder.

"I know," she said, working his jeans down around his hips. He carefully kicked off his boots, wary of the special parcel he hid there, but she wasn't willing to wait for him to be too methodical. The redhead almost ripped off her dress, leaving the tattered garment in limp strings around her waist. Slocum found himself torn between getting his boots off and staring at Florrie's fine body.

She had high, firm snowy breasts capped with taut coppery nipples, a trim waist and flaring, womanly hips. And the tangled brunette mat between her creamy thighs drew his gaze. She saw his attention and laughed demonically. Florrie took a step forward and thrust her bare thigh in his direction, then turned and rotated her hips so she could shove her nether lips into his face.

"Go on, give me what I gave you," she said, her voice shrill. "Use that tongue of yours!" Florrie gasped when Slocum did as she asked.

Slocum reached up and gripped her naked buttocks and pulled her down on top of him. They sank together to the thin mattress, Slocum under the woman's heaving, writhing body. As they struggled together passionately, she slowly slid down his body until her crotch was directly above his painfully hard shaft. Slocum grunted when she reached down and gripped him firmly, then guided him into her most intimate recess.

Slocum grunted in pleasure as he felt her heat surrounding him fully. She lowered her hips and took him balls deep into her center. Reaching up, Slocum cupped her apple-firm breasts. She shoved her chest down hard into his palms and arched her back before howling like a love-sick coyote.

Then Florrie went berserk, her hips flying up and down, twisting and turning around Slocum's fleshy spindle. The heat of her rapid movement threatened his control again. He burned inside and out. He held onto her breasts, crushing them hard, as his hankering grew to match hers. This spurred the woman on to even more strenuous gyrations. Slocum arched his back and shoved himself even deeper into the woman's steamy interior. Then he felt her female sheath clamp down hard all around him, crushing him flat.

He groaned as Florrie howled like an animal again. Her passion knew no bounds. She thrashed about as if she had epilepsy, completely out of control. The woman had turned into a wildcat and was not to be denied. Then she rose, hesitated when only the tip of his manhood remained within her fleece-hidden lips, then crashed down hard into his groin. Slocum thought he could cleave her in two. Instead, Florrie spasmodically panted and shuddered all over, then sank down so she rested her cheek on his chest.

"I was right. You're a real stallion!"

She wiggled her rump a little and disengaged from Slocum's still hard shaft. Florrie had gotten off, but Slocum was left high and dry.

"What about—?" he began, only to see the crazy expression in her coffee-colored eyes again. She shoved him down callously and stood, stark naked, and looked down at him. He had never seen such a bizarre, mad look on a woman's face before.

Slocum *had* seen the look before, however, on a man. A man out of his, mind with hydrophobia and turned kill-crazy.

"Michael, you want to know about Michael," she cried, her voice cracking with strain. "You gave me what I wanted—needed. I'll tell you what you want, but you won't get anything else from me! He was going to a poker game down at Pier 13."

"When?" Slocum struggled with his pants.

"An hour ago, just before I found you in the Sydney Duck!"

Slocum fumbled with his gun belt and took extraordinary care with his boots, not wanting to disturb the package he had crammed in the top for safekeeping. His attention divided between getting on his boots and the increasingly insane-appearing Florrie, he had no chance to stop her when she took a half-step away, pressed her bare back against the wall, then swung open the door and ran into the hall, screeching incoherently at the top of her lungs.

Startled, Slocum finished pulling on his boots and settled his gun belt at his waist. Only then did he follow the buck-naked woman into the narrow hallway, worrying that her shrieking would draw unwanted attention and with it a Special or even a couple policemen. Slocum was only mildly surprised to see that no one had paid Florrie any attention. It was that kind of place.

Quickly going after her, he burst from the bagnio into the cold nighttime street, poorly lit with sputtering gaslights at the end of the block. San Francisco had turned mysterious and veiled in swirling wet gray fog in the few minutes he had been with the woman. He heard Florrie's deranged laughter in the distance, muffled by fog, and started to go after her. Then he stopped dead in his tracks. He had no obligation to her, but he did to Michael Porges.

He made sure his Colt Navy rode easy in its holster, then set off to find Pier 13 and the poker game that had drawn Porges like an ant at a picnic to spilled honey.

2

The cold fog wrapped Slocum like soggy cotton wool. He got lost in the twisting cobblestone streets more than once and had to stop, listen for the baleful ringing of the buoy out in the harbor to get his bearings, and then continue. He found the waterfront and made his way along the shoreline until he came to a rotting pier. At the end of it dangling over the water tottered a saloon, the kind of low dive that Michael Porges might frequent.

Slocum walked gingerly on the decaying wood until he saw a poorly painted sign proclaiming the saloon to be the "Pier 13."

He nodded to himself. Luck rode with him tonight. He had easily found the spot Florrie had mentioned with minimum effort. Slocum might have hunted the pier in the fog all night long before stumbling across it. As it was, he wondered how lucky he could count himself. Just inside the swinging doors he paused and looked around for Porges. The only patrons were seamen, and rough ones by their look.

Slocum knew he had stepped in it when he realized all the sailors wore the same uniform. They came from a single ship, and he was the only non-crew member in the saloon other than the bartender. He licked his lips, tried to make out faces through the thick blue smoke filling the room but could not find Michael Porges anywhere.

Walking slowly to the bar, he leaned against it and ordered a shot of whiskey.

"Never seen you in here before, cowboy," the barkeep said in a neutral tone, as if he didn't want to scare off his customer. The man wore a dirty fox fur patch over his left eye and from the clicking sound as he walked, he had a peg leg. Slocum knew he had only a few minutes before a fight started—a fight he could never hope to win against a tavern full of crew from the same ship.

"I'm hunting for a friend named Porges. A real gambling fool," he said, trying not to appear too concerned at the attention he attracted. "You see him in here tonight?"

"Never heard of him," the barkeep said too fast, taking the greenback Slocum had dropped on the counter.

"He came here for the big poker game."

"Game? What game? Ain't got gamblers in here. All we got on Pier 13's a bunch of tried 'n true sailors!"

This caused a ripple of amusement that drew even more attention to Slocum and his questions. He lifted the whiskey to his lips but didn't toss it back when he saw the gleam in the barkeep's one good eye. The drink was loaded with knockout drops. Slocum put it back on the bar and shook his head.

"Too bad. He owes me money, and I wanted to collect before he lost it."

"Drink up," the barkeep said. "Your buddy might owe you money but you're among friends. Why, I'm so danged friendly, I'll buy you another drink. When you down that one."

Like a rabbit being eyed by a hawk, Slocum again lifted the doctored drink but did not put it to his lips.

"There's no point drinking if my friend's not here to join me. You sure he's not here? In some back room?"

"We ain't got a back room," the barkeep said before he realized what he was saying.

"Guess I have the wrong place for a poker game," Slocum said, putting the whiskey back on the bar and knowing it was time to hightail it.

Slocum started for the door but found his way blocked by a pair of burly salts. He shrugged his shoulders and widened his stance a mite. The men looked into his hard green eyes and saw only tombstones there. They exchanged quick glances, then stepped away to allow Slocum to pass between them. He exited into the cold night and heaved a sigh that he had escaped with his life. Then Slocum realized something was wrong. His hand flashed to his Colt Navy but never got there before a heavy club crashed into the back of his skull.

Slocum stirred, his head full of red hot rocks tumbling around. He touched the back of his neck and winced. His fingers came away bloody from the cut he had sustained. The next thing he reached for was his six-shooter. It was gone.

"You've been shanghaied," came a sullen voice. "Just like the rest of us poor sots."

Slocum realized the darkness was that of a ship's hold. The gentle swaying told him the man was right. He had walked out of the saloon thinking he was safe, only to be cold-cocked when he let down his guard.

"How many are in here?" he asked, feeling a leg near him. The leg's owner recoiled at his touch.

"What's the difference? We're headin' for China come the morning tide."

"You know a man named Porges? Michael Porges?"

"I told you, names don't matter. Nuthin' matters. We're damned! We're damned and sailin' for the Flowery Kingdom!" The shrillness to the man's voice told how close to hysteria he had become.

"I'll get you out of here if you answer my question,"

Slocum said. He touched his vest pocket. The shanghaiers had taken his Colt Navy but had not bothered searching him. He still had a hideout derringer—and the special package in his boot. Together the two would get him off this ship.

"You cain't," the man whined. "Nobody gets away from Captain Greer, nobody. He the toughest damn captain sailin' any clipper ship."

Slocum snorted in contempt. He could get off the ship fast and take any of the men in the hold with him, if they wanted. And if they didn't go along, they would go straight to the bottom of the San Francisco Bay.

"Porges!" he called loudly. "Michael Porges! You in here?"

From his right came a muttering that grew until a gravelly voice answered his call.

"Who wansa know?" Porges was drunk as a lord.

"You want to go home?"

"Home? Hate my father . . .'n her, too. Why go?"

"Unless you prefer going to China as an impressed sailor, get your ass moving," Slocum said. He edged to Porges on hands and knees and moved to the empty pallet next to the man. Slocum lit a lucifer match. In the bright flare, he saw the young man clearly.

He had found Michael Porges.

Slocum heaved himself around and fumbled in his boot, pulling out the red cylinders stuffed there. He had put the two sticks of dynamite there, not sure he would need them or how he might use them. With a sure hand, he drew out the explosive, fastened a blasting cap to the side of one stick and then stuck on a foot of black miner's fuse.

"One foot, one minute. Get yourself ready," Slocum said.

"Fer wat?" Porges slurred his words but seemed to be fighting the effect of too much booze—or a snootful of knockout drops.

"To swim," Slocum said. A second lucifer flared. He applied it to the end of the fuse. It sputtered and cast shadows throughout the hold. The sparks excited the others in the hold. A couple yelled and banged on the grating overhead that they didn't want to be drowned like rats. When one tried to grab Slocum and stop him from tossing the dynamite to the side of the hold, he drew his derringer and shoved it in the man's face.

"Get back," Slocum warned. And then the concussion from the exploding dynamite knocked them across the hold. For a heartstopping second, Slocum thought nothing had happened. Then the side of the ship gave way and water flooded the hold.

"We're sinking. The damned fool blew a hole in the ship! Let us out!" screeched one of the shanghaied men.

On deck above Slocum heard the ruckus. The clipper ship already listed to port side. Slocum grabbed Porges by the collar and pulled him erect. The water came to his waist. Then the crew above unlocked the hatch and threw it back.

"Out!" Slocum cried, shoving Porges ahead of him. The rising water buoyed them and floated them up. Already the crew abandoned ship, diving overboard. On the top deck stood a man in a flashy gold-braided uniform.

"Desertion!" the man cried. "No one deserts Will Greer's ship!"

"So that's Captain Greer," Slocum muttered. He looked around, hoping to see someone with his stolen Colt Navy shoved into a broad belt. The confusion proved too much for such a hunt. Cursing his loss of a decent six-shooter, Slocum shoved Porges toward the railing. The ship already listed forty-five degrees.

"He's the one, Captain!" shouted the man from the hold, pointing at Slocum. "He's the one what blowed the hole in yer boat!"

For a brief instant, Slocum and Greer locked eyes. The

captain's mouth thinned to a line and then he cut loose with a bellow like a scalded pig.

"Over," Slocum said, shoving Porges over the railing and into the water. He hit the dark, freezing cold water and felt the life being sucked from his body. Sputtering, Slocum got to the surface and looked around for Porges. The young man was nowhere to be seen. Thrashing about in a circle, Slocum couldn't find him. Diving into the inky water, Slocum hunted for Porges and found him floating a few feet under the surface.

Grabbing him by the collar, Slocum kicked for the surface, then started swimming with the drowning man in tow.

"Can't go on. No strength," Porges said.

"Swim, damn your eyes," snarled Slocum. He grabbed a piece of flotsam and tugged on Porges until he got him over the broken wood spar. Then he started kicking, pushing the spar with Porges on it toward the distant shore. The clipper ship had anchored some distance from the docks, possibly to keep anyone from noticing the shanghaied men in the hold—as if anyone in San Francisco cared.

"We're almost there," Slocum said, feeling the current around him changing. An undertow threatened to suck him under, but Slocum was determined. It had taken two days to track down Michael Porges, and he was not going to lose him now.

Slocum felt muck under his boots and then he stumbled onto the gravelly shore, dragging Porges after him. Collapsing, Slocum got his breath back. A light breeze blowing off the bay chilled him to the bone, but the sight of Greer's ship going to the bottom warmed him.

"Come on. Get moving. We have a ways to go," Slocum said.

"You saved my life," Porges said, not sober but recovering fast from his ordeal. "They knocked me out and shanghaied me and—"

"Walk," Slocum said. He wanted done with the ne'er-do-well. They reached California Street, crossed to Market, and then cut to the north, plodding along to the Porges mansion up on Nob Hill. The fog had lifted, leaving a clear, cold night to freeze Slocum.

Slocum's discomfort grew as they trudged along. Porges muttered unintelligibly to himself, eyes down and wrapped in his own thoughts. Slocum looked around alertly, wondering what put him on edge. The gaslights hissed and the street stretched empty ahead and behind. Slocum knew because he kept turning around to see if anyone crept up on them. He fingered the derringer and then relaxed a mite. He was jumpy because of the fracas on the boat. It was too late for the strange cable car with its clanking underground wires to run up the hill, and the streets were empty of all life.

Still, he had survived the war relying on his instincts. Slocum pulled out the derringer and cocked it, worrying for the first time if the swim in the harbor might have ruined the double-barreled pistol's mechanism or cartridges.

"What's wrong?" asked Porges, looking up. His bloodshot eyes were curiously flat, showing almost no emotion. Slocum remembered how he had tracked the man through Chinatown's worst dives, the opium dens, and then to the Embarcadero where Porges had tried to drink himself into oblivion. It was nothing short of a miracle that Michael Porges had any awareness left at all after such a bender.

"I don't know this neighborhood, that's all," Slocum lied. "How much farther to your house?"

"My father's house," Porges said bitterly. "I'll never get out from under his thumb, no matter what I do. Why'd you have to come for me? Maybe I'd have been better off going to China. I wouldn't have to listen to Father's sanctimonious lectures that way."

"How far?" Slocum snapped the question now. His sharp ears caught the sound of boot soles scraping on the pavement. They were being followed by someone expert at it. No matter how hard Slocum searched, he could not find their tracker.

"Not that much farther. Just up this hill. We're at the foot of the road leading—" Porges cut off his words abruptly as he stared past Slocum's shoulder. Slocum reacted, rather than consciously thought about what caused the sudden break in the man's directions.

Slocum shoved Porges to one side, lifted the derringer, spun and fired at the dark figure racing on cat's feet at them from across the street. The small pistol made a popping sound unlike the sharp snap Slocum was accustomed to hearing from his Colt Navy. But the round flew straight and true. Or so it appeared, because the dark-cloaked attacker dug in his heels, skidded to a halt, and then turned away slightly, as if injured.

It took Slocum a second to realize the derringer had misfired. The report he heard came from their attacker's gun, a small bore hideout Smith & Wesson Russian model. A curl of white gun smoke crept from the muzzle, verifying Slocum's suspicion as to which of them was the successful gunman.

Slocum cocked the derringer again and fired again. The dull click told him this chamber had misfired, too. But the dark figure bent over and raced away, making hardly any sound at all as he fled. Twice Slocum had fired, and twice his weapon had failed him.

"I don't know why he left. That was a five-shot pistol he had and he saw how the derringer—" Slocum stopped and stared. Michael Porges lay on the hard cobblestones, clutching his belly.

The single shot had found its target, and their assailant had run off because he had succeeded in his deadly mission.

3

Slocum wished he had more rounds for the derringer. For all that, he wanted his Colt Navy back at his hip where it belonged. Lacking both weapons, he knew he could not stay on the San Francisco street any longer without risking the same fate that had been delivered so quickly and unexpectedly to Michael Porges.

He knelt and pressed his fingers down hard onto Porges's chest. A rapid, fluttering heartbeat under the ribs told him the young man was still alive. Barely. Slocum grunted as he heaved Porges up and over his shoulders. Slocum staggered under the man's weight, got his balance, then began walking up the steep street to the houses perched on top of Nob Hill. As he walked, he worried. Porges's attacker could return at any time, and Slocum strained to catch the slightest sound on the pavement behind him.

Nothing. In the distance he heard the noises of the harbor and wished he could see if Greer's ship had been sent to the bottom. Slocum did not turn. Instead, he bent under the weight on his shoulders and kept moving deliberately until he reached the iron gate in front of the Porges mansion. Slocum kicked open the gate and resolutely climbed the steps. Only when he found a decent place to drop Michael Porges, where he might be protected from gunmen out in the street, did he knock on the ornately carved wood front door.

It took several long minutes for a housekeeper to answer. The gray-haired woman rubbed her eyes and then clutched her robe tightly at her throat when she recognized her early morning caller.

"What is it?" she asked in a surly tone. She had been coldly civil when he had met with the elder Porges before, but now dropped all pretense at politeness. Slocum did not blame her. He wouldn't be too cheerful at being awakened this early in the morning, either. After being slugged and shanghaied, then swimming ashore in the filthy harbor, he had to look and smell like a drowned rat.

"Get Mr. Porges. I've found his son, and he's hurt bad."

"Michael?"

"He's on the porch. Where can I put him?"

"In the front room, on the sofa," the woman said, now galvanized into action. She left the door open for him as she hurried up the stairs to the room at the top. The woman knocked insistently on the closed door to the bedroom and spoke in a hushed tone Slocum could not overhear, even if he had tried. He was too busy getting Michael Porges inside and sprawled on the couch in the room looking out over the dark city.

"Where'm I?" muttered Michael Porges.

"Don't talk," Slocum said. "You're home—your father's house. He'll see to getting a doctor for you."

"Shot," Michael said, his hands fluttering to his chest. "Came up and shot me!"

"Drink this," Slocum said, dribbling water from a glass on a nearby table onto Porges's lips.

"What's going on?" Nathan Porges came into the room, larger than life. He was a tall, powerful man, thick of chest and thin of hair. His eyes were sharp and clear and fixed instantly on his son. "Michael!"

"Father?"

"He needs a doctor," Slocum said, "not conversation."

"I've sent Mildred for Doctor Graff. He won't be long."

"Let your son rest," Slocum said, putting himself between Porges and the injured man.

"Very well. Come into the study where you can tell me what's happened." Nathan Porges swept out of the room in a grand exit that left Slocum cold. Porges tried to be dramatic, but Slocum found the railroad tycoon irritating. He sank into one of the expensive chairs, not caring if he stained it with the damp filth from his clothes. Getting Michael home had taken the starch out of his legs.

"Have some brandy," Porges said, indicating a decanter on a table. He made no move to get the drink for Slocum.

Slocum ignored the offer and launched into a description of what had happened, ending with the attack at the foot of the hill.

"Who wants your son dead?" Slocum asked.

"No one, no one at all. That had to be a coincidence. A robber."

Slocum said nothing. They both knew how absurd that sounded. The gunman had made no effort to rob them. The intent had been to rush up, kill Michael, and then leave. If Slocum had been the target, he would have a bullet in his back now. The single-minded attack had focused entirely on Porges's son.

"Why did he go off on this binge?" Slocum asked.

"You did good work, Slocum. You returned him."

"He told me he might have preferred being shanghaied and sent to China as a deck hand rather than come back here. Those are mighty strong words."

"They show Michael is not right in the head," Porges snapped. "He needs my help more than ever. If he wanted hard work among the Celestials, he could join any of my crews laying track in the Sierras." Porges sniffed derisively. "The truth is, he is a confused young man who does not know what he wants."

Slocum let it drop. He was tired and wanted to crawl under a blanket and sleep for a week. The family troubles of the Porges clan were not his concern.

"Here. For your trouble tonight," Porges said. He opened a desk draw, took out a roll of greenbacks, not even bothering to count the bills, and tossed them in Slocum's direction. The crisp new bills fluttered to the desk in front of Slocum. For two cents and a chewed plug of tobacco Slocum would have let the money lie. In a curious way, it struck him as blood money. He was nothing more than a bounty hunter bringing in a criminal for a reward.

He scooped up the money and tucked it in his shirt pocket along with what remained of the soggy money Porges had given him earlier. Porges didn't need the money. He did.

A commotion in the front hall signaled the arrival of the doctor. Slocum saw the small, neat man, presumably Doctor Graff, hurry into the front room and begin his ministrations from a small black leather bag.

"German," Porges said with some distaste. "But a good doctor, nonetheless."

"I'll be going," Slocum said.

"Wait, Slocum, wait. I have been rude. I apologize. Please understand the strain on me caused by my wayward son's return. I want to do something for you that will show my real appreciation."

"I've been paid," Slocum said, touching the thick wad of greenbacks in his shirt pocket.

"Yes, yes, that. But I detect in you something of the Southern gentleman. Given the chance, you know how to behave in polite society. Accept my invitation to join me at the Union Club this evening."

The Union Club was the most exclusive gambling parlor in all San Francisco. Slocum had been there once or twice before and had learned to enjoy the opulence—and the way money flowed like water. Never had he seen worse gamblers, even in the lowest dives along the Embarcadero. The difference was that these men had lots of money and were used to losing it at the gaming tables, calling it entertainment.

"I'll need to find suitable clothing," Slocum said.

"Eight o'clock," Porges said, nodding absently. Then he went to get Doctor Graff's opinion on Michael. Nathan Porges never bothered to show Slocum out, but he did not have to. Slocum was able to find the front door on his own and was even relieved to step out into the chilly predawn wind blowing off the harbor.

He was looking forward to the night of gambling at Porges's club. With a bit of luck, he could turn the money he had been paid into a significant bankroll. Maybe enough to buy a string of Appaloosas up north. A *big* string.

Slocum smoothed nonexistent wrinkles out of his fancy duds as he stood at the front door leading into the Union Club. Twin pillars of marble dwarfed even the titans of industry entering the highly polished wooden portals. A bit self-conscious, Slocum made his way to the doorman.

"My name's Slocum and I'm Nathan Porges's guest tonight."

The doorman did his best not to sniff disdainfully.

"I am sure Mr. Porges would—"

"There you are, Slocum. Don't stand outside dawdling. Come on in!" Nathan Porges waved impatiently at Slocum to enter. Slocum passed the astonished doorman. "Sorry about the mixup but I forgot to tell Jennings you were joining me."

"A good thing you came along when you did," Slocum said. "I'd hate to have bought this tux for nothing."

Porges eyed him critically, then jerked his head in the direction of the main room where roulette tables were crowded with men and women in fine evening dress. Slocum decided he must have passed Porges's inspection because the railroad magnate said nothing more about his clothes. Porges went through the room, leaving behind a small wake of impressed people.

Slocum ignored anyone so easily awed by the man and looked around in search of a poker table and rich men who did not know or care about odds. It did not surprise him that he had his choice of tables. Letting Porges continue to work the room like a politician in search of higher office, Slocum watched the ebb and flow of cards at one table where three men in varying stages of inebriation played.

"Mind if I join you?" Slocum asked after a few minutes.

"You got the money, we got the cards," said the man dealing. "What better combination can there be?" He pointed to an empty chair across the table from him. Slocum settled down and took out the almost five hundred dollars Porges had paid him. Showing his entire stake at the beginning wasn't usually good strategy, but he felt he had to convince the men he belonged and that they ought to let him stay.

Slocum was as good as any man in the room—better— but this was not his world. He knew Porges or any of the others could ask him to leave and it would happen without any question. He glanced around and saw four or five immaculately dressed men who were discreet bouncers. Any ruckus would be quickly and quietly addressed by them.

To Slocum's detriment.

"Seven card stud," the dealer said, shoving a ten dollar chip in as ante. Slocum matched and the play began.

For an hour Slocum kept from losing too much and

even gradually increased his stake. Then the blowout hand came. He showed three queens and had the fourth in the hole.

"Everything," Slocum said, pushing it all into the center of the table. The man who dealt eyed him, then shrugged as if it did not matter.

"Let's see what you got," he said.

"Four queens," Slocum said, waiting.

"You got me. Three tens," came the answer Slocum had anticipated. He raked in his winnings, close to four thousand dollars and stared at it for a moment.

"That's it for me, gentleman," Slocum said. "I'm cashing out."

"What!"

The outburst matched what Slocum might have expected at some bayside dive.

"You can't quit now. You've got to give me the chance to win back some of that. It's mostly *my* money you have in front of you," the dealer said.

"No," Slocum said slowly, standing and getting his money into piles and the chips into stacks for easy cashing. "It was your money. Now it's mine. I won it fair and square." Slocum saw the man's expression turn ugly and knew there was going to be trouble. He carried the derringer but did not want to ventilate the man unless he had to.

"You cheated. You must have to win that much," the man said, his jaw clenching and his fists banging on the edge of the table. Slocum had seen men working themselves up into a killing rage before. This man might have all the money in San Francisco but he was a sore loser.

"Any of you other gents think I cheated?" Slocum looked at the other men who had played and saw only blank stares. They wanted nothing to do with this argument. "I won, fair and square, and any man who says I didn't is a liar."

"You're calling *me* a liar!" The man shot to his feet, overturning his chair.

"Only if you say I cheated at cards," Slocum said coldly. He knew the look, he knew the signs, he knew he was going to have to shoot the man to stop him from pulling out whatever hideout gun he had tucked in his vest pocket. Slocum touched the derringer in his own pocket.

"There you are, darling," came a lilting, cheery voice. "How dare you leave me alone like this for so long!" A vision of feminine loveliness came up and locked her arm through his.

She smiled and then turned to the man who had accused Slocum of cheating.

"You don't mind if I spirit him away, do you, Mr. Ralston? Oh, good, I didn't think so. Do get on with your game."

She tugged insistently on Slocum's arm and guided him away from the table. Softly, she said, "The manager will take care of your chips, Mr. Slocum. Don't worry about your winnings."

"You saved me from a nasty situation," Slocum said. "Thank you."

"And?" she asked, batting her long eyelashes at him.

"Why did you bother?"

"Because I owe you," she said. "With all my life, I owe you."

Slocum didn't know what to say. He had never seen her before in his life and had no idea how he could have won such gratitude from a complete stranger.

4

The young woman clinging so familiarly to his arm was tall and slender and had lustrous shoulder length chestnut-colored hair. Her bright blue eyes sparkled, and she smiled easily as they made their way through the crowded room. She moved lightly, turning and greeting and waving, but Slocum saw that the seemingly random walk across the room had a purpose.

It was a purpose he approved of heartily. The woman guided them expertly through the room to the foyer where they could get away from the card tables and the still angry Ralston.

"He owns the California Bank," the woman said, glancing back into the room where the man pounded his fist on the table and spoke heatedly to three companions. She saw Slocum's perplexed look. "Mr. Ralston. He is a banker and quite well known in town. You might have heard of the Palace Hotel. He built that, also."

"I don't move in those circles," Slocum said. He was still wondering why she had saved his bacon the way she had. If she had not come along when she had, Slocum knew he would have got into a real donnybrook with Ralston, maybe one that ended in someone's death. Consid-

ering Slocum had the derringer, it had been likely that
Ralston would have been the one on the floor bleeding to
death.

But this did not explain the woman's interest. The single comment that she owed it to him made him wonder
even more who she was. "You obviously do belong in a
place like this. Who are you?" he asked bluntly.

"Such a one-track mind," she chided. She clung a little
tighter to his arm as they passed through the marble-
floored foyer of the Union Club and into a sitting room
lined with ornate statuary displayed on carved wood ped-
estals. A few old men slumped in the comfortable chairs,
asleep. Others puffed furiously at cigars, filling the air
with thick blue smoke. The woman's nose wrinkled as
she kept Slocum walking through the room to a large,
deserted library.

Slocum looked around, but the only thing interesting in
the room released his arm and went to perch delicately
on the arm of an overstuffed chair. Something about her
face seemed familiar, but he could not figure out what. If
he had ever seen her before, he would not have forgotten.
No man could forget a woman this fetching.

"My name's Julia," she said, smiling. "Julia Porges."

"Nathan's daughter?"

"Well, yes," she said, looking disgusted. "I am that. I
consider myself more to be Michael's sister, if that makes
any sense."

"It does," Slocum said. He had talked enough with Nathan Porges to know being his son or daughter could not
be too easy.

Julia looked at him for a moment, then laughed. "How
Papa found you is a miracle. Your sense of humor is quite
refreshing. Very dry and biting, without being too overt.
I like that."

"I'm glad," Slocum said. "Anything you like is fine
with me."

"Don't get any ideas, Mr. Slocum," she said, turning serious. "You made a real enemy in Ralston. The man has fallen on hard times, ever since the '73 Panic wiped out many of the San Francisco banks. He acts prosperous, but his wealth is a shadow of its former size. Taking even the paltry few thousand from him as you did makes you his enemy."

"He'd kill me to get it back?"

Julia looked perturbed, then nodded. A wisp of her perfectly coiffed brown hair drifted across her forehead. She pushed it back without realizing she did so.

"There have been rumors of dastardly things Mr. Ralston has done recently. I discount them—some of them. There is no doubt as to his ruthlessness or the degree he is attached to the money in your pocket. I would suggest that you leave San Francisco immediately."

"I was planning on it, anyway," Slocum said, feeling a pang of regret now. Meeting Julia was a stroke of luck, but he *had* intended to drift north and check out the Appaloosa ranches in Oregon. Remaining in San Francisco because of her was not too smart a thing to do, especially in light of Ralston's ire.

Even without the banker being on the warpath, Slocum was enough of a realist to know there could be no future for him with Julia. She was high society and he wasn't.

"Papa paid you well for getting Michael back. I wanted to add my own thanks before you left," she said, coming toward him. Slocum's heart leaped. In spite of there not being a future between them, Slocum was willing to live for the moment. The lovely woman turned her face up slightly and her eyes half-closed, as if she expected him to kiss her. Slocum was willing to be wrong about her intentions. It was easier apologizing if that wasn't what she wanted from him than it was missing such an opportunity.

As he reached for her, the carved wood library door

creaked open. Slocum and Julia jumped apart. From her guilty expression, Slocum knew who had found them. Without turning, keeping his eyes fixed on Julia, Slocum said, "What can I do for you, Mr. Porges?"

"You have eyes in the back of your head, Slocum? Never mind. I see Julia has found you. Why didn't you bring him to me right away, as I told you?" The sharpness in his tone caused Slocum to turn. He was ready to tell Nathan Porges to mind his manners when he saw the woman at the railroad magnate's side.

For a split second, Slocum experienced a giddy feeling that he knew her, also. She was older than Julia, but not by many years. Her short hair carried auburn highlights, making it glow a golden brown. She waved a fan in front of her face, partially hiding it as she peered at him from over the top. The chocolate-colored eyes danced with amusement, a cruel amusement that put Slocum on guard. This was a woman who got what she wanted and used people without regard. She seemed a perfect match with Nathan Porges.

"You are such an oaf, Nathan. You have not introduced me to dear Julia's new . . . plaything." She waved the fan briskly, then lowered it to show her swan-like white throat with the most ornate, diamond-studded necklace around it Slocum had ever seen. The jewelry had cost a fortune.

A huge fortune.

She moved lithely and pretended to look at book titles, but she glanced over her shoulder frequently. The eyes were challenging as they locked on Slocum. He had the feeling of a snake watching a bird before feeding.

"Do I know you?" Slocum asked. The woman's wine-colored velvet dress with the white lace trim was distinctive, as were the small pearls all over the dress. Slocum thought he had struck the mother lode in the card game with Ralston. If he had the cost of this dress riding in his pocket, he could buy more than a few horses up in Oregon. He could buy Oregon itself.

"Why, no, we've never met," she said, waving the fan briskly. "Since Nathan is being such a boor, allow me to make the introductions. I am his wife, Amelia."

"My stepmother," Julia said needlessly. The venom in the younger woman's voice told Slocum more than the words.

"Enough of this lolly-gagging," Porges said. "I've ordered dinner for us in the side dining room. You want to chow down, Slocum, or you want to get back to the gambling?"

"Mr. Slocum was leaving, Papa," Julia said. She bit her lower lip and looked at him, a silent plea in her eyes.

"Nonsense. He's my guest. I invited him to the club. He ought to sample everything it has to offer. It's the least I can do for him since he brought back Michael."

"Yes, we should never forget he brought back dear Michael," Amelia Porges said. Her tone carried much the same venom that her stepdaughter's had. Slocum saw that there was not much love lost in this family. The children resented their father taking such a young wife who might cut them out of their inheritance, and the new wife hated the children for the same reason.

"A private room?" Slocum asked.

"Of course," Porges said in disgust. "I'm not the kind who likes others to watch me eat."

"He eats so fast that he dribbles gravy down his chin," Amelia said, grinning wickedly. Her husband ignored her and impatiently gestured for Slocum to follow.

Slocum looked at Julia, who shook her head in resignation and then offered him her arm again. Together, they followed Nathan and Amelia Porges from the library. Slocum kept an eye peeled for Ralston or anyone who might try to collect blood money for the banker. They made their way down heavily carpeted side halls and went into a dining room that might have been set for the crowned heads of Europe. The fancy bone china, the baroque silverware, the servants hovering at his elbow, all put him off.

Julia stood impatiently beside him, looking aggravated until he came to his senses and seated her at his right. Slocum had been on the trail too long to remember every detail of polite society. More than this, he was caught in the crosscurrents of hatred flowing between the people he was ordered to dine with. He stared across the table at her stepmother, and to Slocum's left Nathan Porges dropped heavily into the chair at the head of the table.

"Waiter, get your ass in gear and bring us our food. I'm starving."

"Oh, Nathan, you are *so* impatient," Amelia said, chastising him. Slocum saw how she goaded Nathan to even more boorish behavior.

"Let him be, Amelia," Julia said.

"My dear, whatever do you mean?" Amelia flattened her fan, then laid it down beside her plate and pointed at the linen napkin until a servant came, opened it, and gently laid it on her lap.

"Enough of this small talk," Nathan Porges said. "I asked you to the Union Club for a reason, Slocum. You like this place?"

"It's very lavish, maybe too much for my tastes," he said honestly. Slocum doubted Porges was in the mood to listen to anything that contradicted what he wanted to hear.

"Lavish," Porges snorted. "That's one word for it. Amelia likes the place. I find it boring as hell. But they got good food." He snapped his fingers and waiters came up with the first course, some thick, creamy soup Slocum could not identify even after he sampled it.

"I want you to work for me full-time, Slocum."

"As a baby-sitter for Michael?" asked Julia. "That is insulting!"

Slocum did not ask who she thought had been insulted.

"I was planning on starting a horse breeding business up north," Slocum said, not going into details Porges was not interested in.

"Horses can wait. I'm offering real money. I need a man who gets things done."

"How would you describe this job?" Slocum asked. He almost complained when a waiter took away his soup before he had finished, only to be brought another course. He looked to Julia for a hint as to how to behave. The young woman clenched her jaw and hardly touched her food as it came and went.

"Bodyguard," Porges said, shoving food into his mouth. His manners were as bad as his wife had suggested, even to dribbling down his chin. Porges never noticed.

"Yours? Your son's?"

"See, Amelia, I told you he'd be interested."

"No, Mr. Porges, I am not," Slocum said. "I'm just curious who you think needs to be watched over most."

"I got me hundreds of men working on my railroad, Slocum. If I wanted anyone to guard my back, I'd bring in a few of those roughnecks. They'd kill a man for a dime. Hell, they'd kill a man just because I asked." Porges shoveled in more food, chewed, belched, and then dropped his fork.

"You want me to look after your son," Slocum said. "I'm not interested."

"It's not as bad as you are making it out, Slocum. Michael's not got any friends. Pal around with him, keep him out of trouble."

"Papa! You mean you're *buying* friends for Michael now? That's outrageous!"

"You keep your mouth shut if you can't keep a civil tongue in your head," Porges said coldly.

Slocum took his napkin from his lap and tossed it onto the table. He stood, peering down at the railroad tycoon.

"That's enough," he said. "Thanks for inviting me here, but you can't pay me enough to baby-sit your son—or listen to you badmouth your daughter."

"You can't talk to me like that!"

"He just did, Nathan," Amelia said. "And I doubt he intends to rush off, north or anywhere else."

"What do you mean, Amelia?" Porges glared at his wife.

"You wondered why Julia did not fetch Slocum right away? The two of them had sneaked off for, how shall I say this delicately? They were engaged in a truly disgusting display of affection. I saw them at it but hesitated to tell you until now. She had his, well, you know, in her mouth."

Slocum and Julia both turned and stared dumbfounded at the woman.

"What are you saying, woman?" demanded Porges.

"I saw them before you found them in the library. In flagrante delicto."

"What are you saying?" Porges's face turned florid with anger. "Is it what I think you're saying?"

"They were engaged in sexual congress, Nathan. Quite perverted, too. I saw them."

"You lying witch!" cried Julia. She knocked her chair over as she shot to her feet. "I only met Mr. Slocum a few minutes before you came into the library."

"So you'd like us to believe. Isn't it convenient he found Michael so easily, Nathan? Perhaps Julia set him on the right path. You know how it is with . . . pillow talk."

"You, you!" Julia sputtered angrily.

Slocum felt a coldness in his belly that spread until it clutched his heart.

"Mr. Porges, I never met your daughter until tonight.

There's nothing between us. I don't know why your wife is saying such things, but I am sure Miss Porges is—"

"Quite the little slut," Amelia said, savoring the insult.

"Papa, are you going to let her say these things about me?"

Slocum saw that Nathan Porges was not about to contradict his wife. Amelia hated Julia, and the feeling was mutual if he read the younger woman's expression accurately. And he would have been blind and dumb not to. Julia shook, her anger barely contained.

This was no place for him. Whatever he said would be twisted by the vicious Amelia Porges. Slocum was sorry to leave Julia in such a pickle, but he doubted it was the first time this had happened. There was bad blood between Julia and her step-mother and it had not just sprung up. It had probably been there ever since it became obvious Nathan Porges was going to marry Amelia.

"Excuse me," Slocum said. "I don't want the job looking after Michael, and I certainly do not want to stay and listen to Miss Porges being vilified like this." He saw the flash of satisfaction on Amelia's lovely face followed quickly by an unabiding hatred directed at him he could not fathom.

For a fleeting instant he almost remembered where he had seen her. Then he pushed it aside. It did no good staying one second longer.

"Go on, get out of my sight before I take a horsewhip to you!" cried Nathan Porges, his face turning red as a beet. "Having your way with my daughter! How dare you, Slocum?"

Slocum paused and started to tell off Porges, then knew it would do no good.

"Good evening, Miss Porges," he said to Julia, then cashed his chips and left. Just outside the dining room, Slocum paused. Ralston and three disagreeable-looking men blocked the front door.

5

John Slocum considered bulling his way past Ralston and the men with him, then decided against it. He didn't have the high ground for this fight. Ralston belonged to the Union Club and was well-known in San Francisco as both banker and hotelier. He might be skirting bankruptcy, but he was still richer than Slocum would ever be and his word carried considerable weight among those he lent money to and put up in his posh hotel.

Sidling along the plastered wall, Slocum slipped back into the main casino. With Ralston and his well-dressed highbinders blocking the front door, that meant Slocum had to find the rear exit and get out that way. He circled the room, keeping close to the wall to be sure no one came up behind him. As he reached the far side of the casino he looked across the room and saw Julia Porges frantically hunting.

For him, he guessed. Slocum felt sorry he had left so suddenly, but if he had gotten embroiled in the Porges family squabble, he would have ended up with everyone mad at him. One thing he had learned about such disputes was that any third party butting in always got blamed for everything. He was happy enough leaving Michael on the mend and Julia with some vague appreciation for his efforts.

Julia waved at him and came through the room. As the lovely woman got halfway to him, a card game ended and the five men rose, blocking her way. Slocum figured Julia would be good at wending her way through such human blockades, so he hurried on to the small door he had spotted at the rear of the main room. He slipped through the door and walked down a service corridor so narrow his shoulders brushed both walls. Rooms on either side held supplies and, at the end of the corridor, he found himself in the Union Club kitchen. Waiters bustled about with trays of food and cooks toiled over hot stoves to make the elaborate concoctions demanded by the club members.

"Only passing through," Slocum said when a startled chef started for him with a cleaver in his hand. Giving the chef no chance to respond, Slocum ducked out the rear servants' entrance into the cold San Francisco night. A stiff breeze blew across Alcatraz Island with its federal prison and chilled him doubly.

He doubted Ralston could send him to the prison but did not want to trust the California courts, should the banker decide not to settle the matter personally. The money was better in Slocum's pocket than in Ralston's— and Slocum had won it fairly. He felt nothing but contempt for the man, trying to welch on the bet.

"Can't afford to lose, don't bet," Slocum muttered to himself as he started walking. He knew he attracted attention from the grounds staff. Patrons of the Union Club gussied up in their tuxedos seldom left on foot. Slocum had the money to hail a carriage but to do so gave Ralston a trail to follow.

Slocum reached the foot of the hill and looked around, wondering what to do now. Again he wished he wore his Colt Navy. Back in his hotel room he had a spare, but wearing it to the Union Club had been out of the question.

Somehow, the derringer gave him no sense of confidence. Two shots out of the short barrel were nowhere as good as six rounds from his Colt.

Being on foot in San Francisco after dark was always chancy. Wearing his monkey suit marked him as a target for any footpad or highbinder who spotted him. If he had wanted to avoid Ralston and his thugs, he certainly wanted to avoid the lower class killers willing to stab him in the back simply to steal his shoes.

Slocum faded into the shadow of a doorway and waited, fuming at the delay. He wanted to get back to his hotel off Union Square, pack and get to the livery so he could ride out of town immediately. Every second ticking by struck him as one less second he had to live. Going to the Union Club at Porges's behest had been profitable enough, but it had brought down the wrath of the minor deities of San Francisco society on his head.

He frowned, trying once more to remember where he had seen Amelia Porges. Something about her eyes reminded him of—

Slocum jerked alert and stepped out when a carriage rattled past, heading up the hill toward the Union Club.

"Taxi!" he shouted, waving his hand in the air. He caught the hackney driver's attention. The man started, then relaxed a mite when he saw how Slocum was dressed.

"You needin' a ride, sir?"

"I surely do," Slocum said, climbing in. He sank back on the hard seat, then slid down so he wouldn't be easily seen by anyone on the street. He heaved a sigh of relief when he got the driver turned around and heading for his hotel.

It took forever to reach Union Square, or so it seemed to Slocum. He paid the driver, then hurried to the hotel's front door, only to find it locked. Slocum banged on the door but could not rouse the clerk inside. He looked around the deserted plaza and then decided his only hope of getting into the hotel lay in finding an open back door. He circled the building, finding a debris-strewn alley behind the hotel.

"At last, Lady Luck's on my side," he said, seeing a partially open door. Light from inside the hotel spilled into the dark alley, a beacon showing him the way to safety.

As he started down the alley, he heard horse's hooves clattering on the pavement behind him. Slocum half-turned, saw his danger, then dived for cover as a bullet ripped past his head. He hit hard, rolled, and came to a sitting position, his back against the hotel's rear brick wall. Slocum fumbled out his derringer, cocked it, and fired at the horse's rider.

Instincts honed over the years warned Slocum he had missed his attacker. He cocked the derringer again and prayed the single remaining round would stop the attack.

The rider's horse reared, then charged forward. Slocum lifted his derringer and aimed at the indistinct figure. A darkly flowing cloak obscured his target and made a killing shot difficult. Even worse, Slocum found himself dodging new bullets sent in his direction. He winced as a bullet ripped through his fancy duds and creased his side. The sudden pain caused him to jerk off his shot.

It went wild.

Then the horse with its rider flashed past, thundering down the alleyway toward the far side of the hotel.

Slocum forced himself to his feet, trying to ignore the pain in his side. The wound was shallow but it bled like a stuck pig. He pressed his hand against his ribs and staggered toward the open door. Before he reached it, he saw the rider was not content with a single attack. The rider wheeled around and galloped at him once more.

The derringer carried two spent rounds, and Slocum had no time to reload. The short barrel and dubious ballistics made firing again at a target more distant than a foot or two a matter of faith rather than skill.

New rounds spanged off the brick wall around Slocum's head. He ducked, got his legs under him, and then launched himself through the open door. Hitting the kitchen floor, he skidded and crashed into a cabinet. Momentarily stunned, he watched helplessly as the rider stopped outside the door. Slocum could see the six-shooter pointed straight at his head. The click as the hammer fell almost caused his heart to explode.

Then he realized the hammer had fallen on an empty chamber. His attacker was out of ammo, too. Heartened by this, Slocum got to his feet and stumbled toward the door. The rider must have thought he intended to pursue the fight. Spurs flashing in the dim light from the kitchen, the rider savagely gouged the horse's flanks, causing the animal to rear and paw the air to keep Slocum at bay.

Slocum had no intention of fighting the rider—the rider who reminded him greatly of the man who had shot Michael Porges. He grabbed the door and slammed it hard. Quick moves slammed the locking bolts on the top and bottom of the door and gave Slocum sanctuary.

Panting harshly, he leaned against the door. From the alley he heard the thud of hooves receding into the distance.

"What you do in my kitchen?" demanded an old Chinese man. "You breed! No breed on my crean froor!"

Slocum shook his head, clearing it.

"Sorry," he said, seeing the man was right. A line of bloody drops ruined the cleaning job. "Here, take this. Sorry for the trouble." Slocum shoved a ten dollar greenback into the man's hands. The Celestial bobbed his head, then motioned for Slocum to get the hell out.

Slocum was glad to oblige.

He made his way through a rat's maze of halls and eventually found the back stairs leading to the third floor.

Constant pressure on his wound kept it from bleeding more. By the time he reached his room and shucked off the ruined tuxedo, the wound had caked over. It pained him as he twisted around but otherwise did not seem serious. Slocum took a few minutes to probe and clean it, then bandaged it with strips torn from his fancy ruffled formal shirt.

"Might as well serve some good purpose," Slocum grumbled. He cast aside the rest of his tux and then dressed in his rough trail clothes, feeling better for it. He felt even better when he took out his spare Colt Navy, then loaded and settled it into his cross-draw holster where it belonged.

Slocum stretched cautiously, testing the limits of his body now that he carried the bloody wound on his side. He could use his six-gun just fine. He had better avoid getting into a fistfight for a few days until the injury healed a little, though.

Hastily packing his gear, Slocum slung the saddlebags over his shoulder, grimaced a bit at the pang in his side, then headed down the stairs to the lobby. The night clerk snored noisily behind the counter. Slocum reached over and took the front door key without waking him, then unlocked the door and stepped back into the cold San Francisco night.

He almost expected his attacker to be waiting, but the expanse across Union Square was empty. He set off for the livery stable a few blocks away along Market Street, his boots crunching on the gravel littering the cobblestone street. With every step he took, he glanced around. Slocum quickly grew tired of such useless vigilance and picked up the pace to reach the stables.

The owner slept in the house adjoining the stables. Slocum had paid, through the end of the week and saw no reason to rouse the man.

"Somebody ought to get some sleep tonight," he grumbled. The side door was locked but Slocum pulled the hasp loose and went inside. Half the stalls were full and horses whinnied uneasily at his entry. He went to the stall closest to the double doors leading out the front and gentled the sorrel there.

"It's time to get out of San Francisco," he told the horse. "I'll get you saddled up and . . . we can go," he finished. The noise behind him warned that he was not alone with the horses. Slocum kept talking gently to his horse as he moved around, then went for his six-shooter, drew, cocked it, and aimed smoothly.

Only Slocum's quick reflexes kept him from shooting Julia Porges.

"John!" The chestnut-haired beauty put a hand to her mouth when she saw he had leveled his six-gun at her. "It's me. Don't shoot!"

"What are you doing here?" he asked, letting the hammer down gently and shoving his six-gun back into his holster.

"Why, we did not part well. I . . . I wanted to say good-bye properly."

"How did you find me?" he asked bluntly.

"It wasn't hard. Papa knew you stabled your horse here. He might own the livery. I don't know for sure."

"He knew the hotel I was staying at, too, didn't he?"

"I suppose so. Yes, he did. He mentioned it, but I thought it best to see if you had already gone, so I came here directly."

"How?"

"I'm sorry. What do you mean?" Her blue eyes blinked in confusion. He might have seen a lovelier woman but he could not remember when or where.

"How did you come here? Ride?" Slocum hated being so suspicious but masked riders shooting at him made him edgy. The slight twinge he felt in his side reminded him how close he had come to being gunned down, too.

"A buggy. I left it outside," Julia said, pointing vaguely behind her. "Do you want me to take you somewhere? I thought from the way you acted this was your horse, but if you want, I can—"

"Let me see," Slocum said. Julia frowned, then turned and preceded him to the door he had broken open. She slipped outside and went around the barn toward the rear where a horse nervously shifted weight from one side to the other. As Julia had said, the horse was hitched to a buggy.

"Sorry," Slocum said. "It's been a confused night."

"Yes, it has. I'm so sorry about my stepmother. She is such a, such a—"

"Bitch," Slocum said, knowing Julia was too refined to come out and say the obvious.

"Yes, that," she said, blushing a little. She lifted her eyes to him and stepped closer until he could smell the heady scent of her perfume. "I am very appreciative of what you did for Michael."

"Your pa paid me for it."

"He buys people as if they are nothing more than wooden railroad ties or Pullman cars. I am *truly* appreciative. No one gives Michael any consideration, and I think you did. And not because you were being paid, either. You did it because you are kindhearted."

Slocum snorted derisively. She did not know him, and he told her that.

"You are trying not to cast a bad light on all those people who are after you," she said. "Ralston is a poor loser, and Papa is cruel. I think I hate him sometimes."

"Like your brother?"

"Yes, like Michael." Julia chewed on her lower lip and then said, "And there was someone else asking after you at the club. The manager chased him away, but he was definitely looking for you."

"Who was it?" Slocum wondered if the masked gunman had tried to get into the Union Club before attacking him in the alley.

"Someone said he was a clipper ship captain named Greer."

Slocum heaved a deep sigh. He had hoped to avoid the furious sea captain, but it sounded as if Greer was hot for his blood, too. Slocum doubted the sailor could ride as well as the gunman in the alley, so that added to the list of those wanting his scalp.

Ralston. Porges. Greer. The unknown rider who had tried to kill Michael and him. It was certainly time to leave San Francisco far, far behind.

"Did I upset you, John?"

"You only confirmed what I thought. Everyone in San Francisco wants to put a bullet into my carcass."

"I wouldn't say that," she said, moving even closer. Her taut breasts crushed into his chest. Julia tipped her head up again, as she had in the library. Her eyes half-closed, and her lips parted slightly. Slocum had wanted to kiss her before. He did so now.

He had wondered if he misread her intentions. Slocum quickly found he had not. Julia threw her arms around his neck and pulled him to her hard. Her lips crushed into his passionately as she moved, grinding her body into his. When her tongue snaked out and dueled erotically with his, Slocum knew he wasn't going to leave San Francisco yet.

He held her tightly, turning around a little. The pressure of her hot body against his drove away the cold night breeze whipping off San Francisco Bay. Panting, Slocum broke off the kiss.

"Let's go into the stables," he said.

"What? And scare the horses?" Julia giggled like a young schoolgirl, then took Slocum's hand and pulled him behind her. "Let's do it!"

They went back into the stables and found an empty

stall with fresh, clean straw on the floor. Slocum grabbed a horse blanket and threw it down. He turned to the woman and found she had not waited while he prepared their bed. Julia had stripped off her blouse and shucked off the clinging undergarment beneath, leaving her delightfully bare to the waist.

Slocum sucked in his breath as he stared at her nakedness. Her breasts were perfect creamy cones capped with coppery plains. The cherry-red nipples in the middle of those plains visibly pulsed and grew firm as her arousal grew.

He pulled her to him, bent and sucked in one rubbery nip. His tongue pressed down into the hard little button and then pushed it around into the softness beneath. Julia moaned with desire and shoved her chest out, trying to get more of her breast into his mouth. Slocum obliged. He reached around and cupped her buttocks, kneading the firm, round globes like loaves of dough as he mouthed her breast.

"Yes, John, so good, so nice, oh, oh!"

He switched to the other creamy cone, his tongue dragging down one slope and up the other to snare the rigid nipple he found waiting for him there. Julia's trim body trembled as he continued to squeeze her rump and suckle at her breast.

Somehow, she managed to lift her skirts. Slocum shifted from her behind to the sleekness of her exposed legs. He ran his hand up and down her thighs and then moved into the secret warmth between. The fleecy mound was damp and ready for him.

"You sure you want to do this?" he asked.

"Stop talking, John, stop talking and get on with it. I want you so!" She clung to him, her arms around his head to keep his face pressed to her chest. Julia twisted and turned and managed to step out of her skirts, leaving her naked as a jaybird. Slocum fell back to sit on the blanket and stared up at her. His heart hammered at the sight of such feminine beauty.

Long legs, trim waist, firm breasts, full lips, Julia had it all. She stepped forward and pressed her crotch into his face.

"Do the same here as you did higher," she said. The woman gasped when he willingly obeyed. His tongue raked wetly over her most sensitive flesh and tasted her oily inner juices. Then the woman's legs buckled and she carried him down the blanket.

"You're overdressed for this occasion," she said, her words coming in gasps. Julia fumbled at his shirt and gun belt and buttons at his fly. Together they worked until Slocum had stripped off the clothing he had only recently changed into.

"What happened?" she asked, finding his bandaged ribs. He flinched as she lightly touched the wound.

"Nothing to worry yourself over," he said, reaching out to draw her down beside him on the blanket. Julia started to protest, but Slocum stifled her questions with his mouth. Their bodies moved alongside each other, rubbing and stimulating. Their hands explored and their mouths communicated without words.

Then Slocum could stand it no longer. He was hard and ready. When Julia reached down and gripped his manhood, he knew there could be no holding back. Pushing her flat onto her back, Slocum rolled between her sleek thighs. His steely shaft brushed against the chestnut thatch and parted her nether lips. Then Slocum levered forward, slipping easily into her.

For a moment, the world stopped around Slocum. Her female sheath clamped down firmly on him, squeezing and massaging and gripping damply at him. Then his hips exploded in a frenzy of activity. He pistoned back and forth, driving deeper, harder, faster. Heat built in his loins. He felt the woman responding to him.

"Oh, oh!" she gasped out, clutching at him. Her fingernails dug into his flesh. This prompted Slocum to arch his back and sink ball's deep into her, trying to split her in half. She groaned, sobbed and ground her crotch into his.

This set off the fiery explosion that built deep inside and gushed forth. Spent, Slocum sank down and then rolled off the woman. Her face was flushed, and she was covered with sweat from their passionate lovemaking. Julia stared at him with bright blue eyes.

"I'm sorry," she said, "that you're leaving town. It could have been so good."

"What?" Slocum said, startled. "I thought it *was* good."

Julia smiled wickedly and said, "I meant the second time."

Her hand reached down and caught at his limp organ. Slocum soon found that she was right. It was better the second time. And then it was time for him to leave San Francisco. Reluctantly.

6

Riding into the pale dawn left Slocum feeling empty inside. He liked Julia Porges as much as he disliked the rest of her family. Her brother would never learn to look after himself, her father was a tyrant who used money as a sledgehammer to get what he wanted, and Amelia Porges was, as Julia had skirted saying, a bitch. Amelia had married rich and intended to keep the money, in spite of her stepchildren.

But Slocum wished he could have spent more time with Julia. Their parting had been bittersweet because both knew they lived different lives and they had no future together. Slocum could never stand San Francisco more than a week or two. There were too many people, too much law, and society making claims on him he refused to honor. Trying to imagine Julia astride a horse all day or living on a ranch or farm was equally absurd. She was a delicate flower with a center of steel perfectly in tune with San Francisco society but out of place cooking dinner on a ranch in Oregon.

More than this, every man with a gun was out after Slocum's hide. For all he knew, Ralston had put a bounty on his head and Greer might intend to work him to death on a ship going to China, should he find and shanghai him.

He heaved a deep sigh, reined back, and waited for the ferry agent to wave him aboard. The wallowing barge slowly crossed San Francisco Bay to the east, cutting off a day or longer ride to the south, skirting the shoreline, and then coming to Port Costa. Slocum needed to get away from San Francisco and all the men out after his scalp and had the money to pay the dollar freight demanded by the ferryman.

Slocum stood at the rail and watched as the San Francisco ferry building at the foot of Market Street slowly dwindled in size until he could no longer read its clock. When he had parted with Julia, it was final. He would never see her again—and that might be for the best. She needed to get on with her life, perhaps helping Michael, probably cutting the apron strings of greenbacks used by her father to hold her to his will and venturing out on her own.

He turned and looked at the approaching Port Costa dock and wondered if he could get as much as thirty miles behind him before nightfall. Dawn poked pearly fingers above the mountains farther east and tried to take some of the wet chill out of the air. Slocum led his horse to the front of the ferry and was first off. He got the lay of the land and found a street running parallel to the bay, heading north to Oakland.

The longer he rode, the better Slocum felt about leaving. With the money he had earned from Porges and won from Ralston, he could buy a remuda of Appaloosas that would make him wealthy in a couple seasons. He knew horses and with a little luck could double the size of his herd in a year.

Buildings became fewer and farther between and more trees popped up, telling Slocum he was getting away from civilization. He sucked in a deep breath and, as he did so, he heard the all-too-familiar click of a cocking six-shooter. Without thinking, he threw himself to the side and grabbed at his sorrel's neck.

The bullet whizzed through the air where his head had been only a fraction of a second earlier.

His horse balked, then reared in fright. Slocum felt his seat slipping. He got his right foot free of the stirrup and then kicked hard to get off the bucking horse. Hitting the ground hard, he rolled and came to his knees. Before, he had been armed only with the two-shot derringer. Now he had a respectable weapon to defend himself.

He whipped out his Colt Navy, cocked it in a smooth movement, and fanned off two rounds in the direction of his attacker. Slocum couldn't even see who shot at him. The shots were intended to either flush the sniper or cause him to duck so Slocum could get to cover.

Slocum saw the gun barrel poke around the side of a dilapidated building across the street. He stayed on his knees but aimed his six-gun carefully this time. When the hand holding the gun appeared, Slocum began firing. His first shot missed. The second caught the side of the gunman's pistol, knocking it from his hand. Quickly following the flying gun came a stream of cussing vitriolic enough to burn the ears off a sailor.

Getting his feet under him, Slocum advanced warily. He had seen some gunmen who carried two six-shooters and even a few who could use them both at the same time. He spun around the corner, his trigger finger tense and ready to fire.

"Git those hands up in the air," came a cold command from behind. Slocum cursed under his breath. How had he let the sniper get behind him? Or had there been two of them coming after him?

Then it hit him. The gunman had tried to backshoot him. If the man behind him had any intention of killing him, he would have fired rather than spoken.

"Somebody tried to gun me down. That's his six-shooter over there on the ground," Slocum said, not raising his hands and judging his chances.

"You're disturbin' the peace, and I *hate* that."

"You the law?"

"Marshal Dawes, if it means a danged thing to you. Now git that hogleg put away and reach for the sky."

Slocum slowly obeyed. He cast a quick glance along the side of the rundown building to make sure he was not turning his back on his would-be killer, then turned to face the marshal. A shiny silver badge on the man's chest gleamed in the morning sunlight. Slocum heaved a sigh of relief. The marshal might be a crook and a bounder, but he was a real lawman.

"Don't go gittin' ideas on reachin' fer that fancy six-gun of yours," Dawes said.

"The man who tried to dry-gulch me is getting away, Marshal."

"So you say." Dawes spat, then circled Slocum, keeping his old black powder Remington aimed at his prisoner's gut. He knelt by the gun Slocum had shot out of the ambusher's hand. "Surely did ruin a fine piece of iron," the marshal said. He spat again. He also shoved his Remington into his jacket pocket.

"I could have caught him," Slocum said, his anger mounting now. "Let me track him. I winged him, so he might be leaving a blood trail."

"You're not gonna do any sich thing," Marshal Dawes said. "You been a bad boy, disturbin' the peace on this fine Sunday mornin'. I don't cotton to anybody doin' that. Makes the churchgoers uneasy, and if they git uneasy, they kick me out of office. Truth is, I like bein' town marshal here in Oakland."

"What are you going to do about the shooting?" Slocum asked.

"Could fling you into the calaboose," Dawes said, as if

actually considering it. "You made a heap of noise, and nobody likes that on a Sunday mornin'."

"I was the one who was shot at!"

"So you say, so you say," Dawes went on. He bit off a bit more from his plug of tobacco and chewed a few seconds to get the juices flowing before he spat again. "Now I kin put you behind bars, or you can jist ride on."

Slocum wondered who had shot at him. Ralston might have sent out killers both south along that trail and across the bay to wait for Slocum. From San Francisco those were the only two ways to get out of town. Thinking on it, Porges could be responsible, also, goaded on by his wife. Porges had been free with information about where Slocum had stayed and even where he stabled his horse.

Or so Julia said. Could the lovely woman be responsible for this attack? Slocum didn't see how she benefited from him getting ventilated, and she had certainly been enthusiastic when they were making love. But with the Porges family, Slocum was beginning to think anything might be possible.

"I was on my way north when I was shot at," Slocum said. "There's no reason I can't get back on my horse and keep riding."

Dawes nodded slowly, rubbed his stubbled chin as he thought on it, spat, and finally said, "That sounds like a good deal for both of us. I don't have to feed you in my jail and you leave whatever trouble you're in behind you."

Slocum waited a few more seconds to be sure Dawes was actually letting him go, then fetched his sorrel and soothed her for a few minutes. The whole time, Marshal Dawes watched him like a hawk. Slocum mounted, touched the brim of his hat in the lawman's direction, then rode on his way, wondering who the hell had tried to kill him and if they would try again.

• • •

Tall trees surrounded him. Here and there grew coastal redwoods, not the big inland ones, but certainly tall enough to satisfy Slocum. The heady odor was completely different from San Francisco or any other town. This was fresh, clean, vital. The stench of gaslights and streets filled with horse manure and other decaying matter, open sewers, and too many people crowded together were a distant memory for him now. He was back where he belonged.

All day he had ridden and not once had he detected anyone on his trail. Slocum had doubled back a couple times, laid low and waited, even raced ahead, found high ground and studied his back trail to see if his attacker from Oakland came after him. He was delightfully alone on the trail north toward Yreka, and that suited him just fine.

But not quite alone. Slocum canted his head to one side when he thought he heard a distant cry for help. Then he was certain he had heard the call when the sharp crack of a rifle reached his ears.

He looked behind him, then slowly swiveled in the saddle and faced north, ahead on the trail. The commotion came from the north. Slocum saw no way for anyone in Oakland to get around him when he had been so vigilant. Slocum realized not all shooting in California was likely to be aimed at him, as much as it seemed that way for the past few days. He juggled his options. He could simply dismount, fix camp, and let the feud ahead die down without getting involved. He could ride back along the trail or cut into the forest and circle the commotion.

Or he could investigate.

This wasn't his fight, whatever it was, but Slocum felt an obligation if someone needed help. He checked his Colt Navy and made sure all six chambers were loaded, drew his Winchester from the saddle sheath, and checked its magazine, then levered in a round and urged his sorrel onward.

The road he had followed all day was cut by a larger one, one with deep ruts showing heavy wagons occasioned it. More shouts and heavy gunfire from up the road told him things were getting tense. He rode slowly, keeping alert for a trap. The road swung around and the trees thinned into a clearing.

A stagecoach had broken down in the middle of the clearing. The shotgun messenger fired repeatedly at a half dozen masked men riding around and around the stage, slowly turning the Concord to kindling wood with their bullets. Slocum saw the driver poke his head up and timidly fire a six-shooter at the bandits before ducking back into the driver's box.

Two gun barrels poked out from the stage, showing armed and dangerous passengers. Slocum considered what he might do to help and decided there wasn't a hell of a lot he could do. The driver and guard were doing a good job keeping the highwaymen at bay. With the sporadic firing from the passengers, the robbers might give up and ride away at any instant.

Slocum hefted his rifle and fired when one of the masked men broke off from the circle around the stagecoach and galloped toward him, six-gun firing. The robber's bullets went wide but still spooked Slocum's sorrel. Using his knees, Slocum got the horse under control, pulled the rifle hard into his shoulder and fired. He shot off the highwayman's floppy black felt hat but otherwise did nothing to slow the man.

Slocum fired again and forced the robber to veer off into the woods. Seeing one of their amigos fleeing caused the others to give up on the attempted robbery. Slocum fired after one of the departing robbers, then lowered his rifle, feeling good about his part in defending the stagecoach.

He jerked around and looked back down the road when he heard horses' hooves pounding like an earthquake. A dozen men waved six-shooters in the air and shouted crazily. Slocum's horse bolted, forcing him to drop his rifle and jerk hard on the reins to slow its frightened gallop.

As he got the horse under control, he found himself surrounded by the riders.

"Whoa, wait!" Slocum called when he saw they all had their guns pointed at him. "I'm no robber. The gang left, hightailed it into the woods. That way." He pointed and nearly got shot.

"Hold on, he ain't got a gun out," bellowed the man who seemed in charge.

"He dropped his rifle tryin' to get away, Gus. Here it is."

The man called Gus took the rifle and sniffed at it. "Been fired. Hell, the barrel's still hot to burn your fingers. He's one of them robbers."

"I was trying to drive them off. Ask the driver or the guard. They must have seen what was going on. I just rode up and——"

"Shut up, you thieving son of a bitch," snapped Gus. "As a duly authorized officer of the court and a Pinkerton officer in good standing sworn to protect this here stagecoach, I hereby arrest you."

"What?" Slocum stared in disbelief. "It's like I told you. Ask the driver or shotgun messenger. Maybe one of the passengers saw me shooting at the road agents."

A Pinkerton man rode back from the stage. He glared at Slocum, as if he wanted to put a bullet in him then and there. "Yep, Gus, he's one of 'em. The driver said so."

"That coward had his head buried so far down in the box, he couldn't see anything!" protested Slocum, growing apprehensive. These might be Pinkerton detectives but they also had the look of a lynch mob about them. Slocum guessed they might have been recruited by a real agent who sat in his office and collected a fat salary from the stagecoach company and then doled out the bounty a little at a time to men like these, men more comfortable hanging around bars and getting drunk.

Men who were more inclined to act as judge, jury and executioner than to return him to a town so he could explain.

"No shootin' him, not till we get him back to Santa Rosa," Gus said.

"I don't want to go to Santa Rosa," Slocum said.

"You ain't got a choice, you miserable thief. We caught you red-handed, and you're gonna stand trial."

Slocum started to turn. He never saw the rifle barrel swinging through the air, but he felt it crack into the back of his head. Slocum wobbled in the saddle, pain shooting through his head like lightning bolts. The second blow coming from a different Pinkerton knocked him from the saddle.

Dark. Everywhere he looked it was dark. For a moment, Slocum thought he had died and gone to hell. Then his head cleared a little and he began to hear and see and smell the world around him. Pine needles crushed under him as he sprawled on the ground told him he was still in the forest. Distant night birds called to one another and a wolf howled in the distance. When his vision finally firmed up and stopped showing double images, he saw the Pinkerton agents crouched at a campfire, swilling coffee and joking with each other.

He tried to move and found himself unable to. Chains at his ankles rattled and alerted Gus that his prisoner had recovered.

"So you're back among the living, eh?" Gus said.

"Not for long. The judge is sure to hang the son of a bitch," another Pinkerton piped up.

"Why wait for the damned judge? You know how he hems and haws and takes forever to get around to sentencing. Let's just string him up now," said another.

"None of that," Gus warned, but not too vehemently. "We're officers of the court *and* Pinkertons. That makes us special. We always bring in our prisoners alive."

"Yeah, but after," insisted another. "What about when the sheriff locks him up?"

"What we do on our own time is our business," Gus said. He poked Slocum with a pointed stick he had recently used to stir the campfire coals. "We might take it into our heads to lynch you."

Slocum winced. Gus had found the shallow bullet wound in his side with unerring viciousness.

"You want to confess and save the town of Santa Rosa the cost of tryin' you?"

"Yeah, mister, confess so we can hang you from yonder scrub oak so we kin git on back to our families."

"Families?" laughed another. "I got a thirst so powerful not even that special bottle behind the bar at the Silver Stallion will quench it!"

The men laughed. Slocum stayed quiet, not wanting to goad them to action. He was lucky they didn't have a bottle to pass around. Dutch courage would push them into hanging him. As it was, they still took some pride in being Pinkertons and upholding the law, even if they didn't quite agree with its letter.

Head hurting, Slocum lay back down and tried to think. Letting the posse take him to Santa Rosa was out of the question. They had already convicted him. He heard Gus go back to the warmth of the fire, swapping lies and tall tales with the others. Trying not to move too much Slocum checked the shackles they had used on his ankles.

Hope surged. They might call themselves Pinkertons but they lacked any training or even common sense. It would take him less than a minute to get free of the shoddily applied chains.

Slocum closed his eyes, catnapping until after midnight. He rolled to one side and studied the men. Most were curled up in their bedrolls. Two who were supposed to be standing guard, sat hunched over, snoring loudly. He sat up, fiddled with the chains for a few minutes and finally got them free.

The rattle of chain links made Gus stir. Of the posse, he seemed to be the one with the most sense. Or maybe he had the most honor, taking his oath as a Pinkerton detective more seriously than the others. Slocum didn't care. All he wanted was to get away.

He got to his feet and walked softly through their camp. He searched the piles of equipment until he found his Colt Navy and returned it to his holster. Of the stack of rifles, his Winchester was easily the best. On impulse, Slocum filled his pockets with as much ammo as he could. The Pinkertons owed him something for the trouble they'd put him through.

Stepping over a sleeping Pinkerton, Slocum went to the rope corral they had fashioned and found his sorrel. The horse was glad to see him, but the other horses neighed and shied from him.

Slocum saddled up and mounted. No one in the Pinkerton camp had noticed he was gone. Yet.

But they would when they woke. He considered spooking their horses, but that would start them on his trail right away.

Anything would start them after him, because they were certain he was a highwayman. He sat astride his horse, thinking hard. Porges and Ralston and Greer might be after him, but he had probably outrun them when he left Oakland. But these were locals, and they had the yen for glory burning brightly in them. Slocum had seen it before.

That and the lust to spill some blood would keep them on his tail until they caught him or he killed them. As satisfying as that might be for Slocum, he was no cold-blooded killer. Killing them in self-defense was not much better and only riled real Pinkertons whose reputation was one of implacable pursuit until they caught their quarry.

Slocum shook his head. There was one way to get rid of the Pinkertons without leaving behind a path of blood and death. It irked him that he had to do their job for them, but bringing in the real robbers was the only way for him to ride on a free man.

He walked his sorrel from the camp, heading for the clearing where the stagecoach had been ambushed. He had to wait until almost dawn for enough moonlight to pick up the robbers' trail.

7

The trail was as plain as the nose on his face, but Slocum
began to slow as he tracked. Something bothered him
about the place where the robbers had attacked the stagecoach, and he could not figure what it might be. When
dawn showed the trail more clearly, Slocum dismounted
and studied the hoofprints in the soft forest dirt.

He identified two different horses by the variations in
their shoes. One had a deep notch in a front horseshoe.
The other had been mis-shod, causing the horse to favor
that leg slightly. Two other riders joined the pair Slocum
followed. That made four. Had the robber coming for him
been a fifth? He had to know how many men he went up
against so he could make a clean sweep.

Slocum realized it might be dangerous taking the gang
in to the sheriff in Santa Rosa, but he was willing to give
it a try to stay clear of a posse willing to chase him across
the entire West. The Pinkerton National Detective Agency
credo was that they always got their man. Slocum had
enough wanted posters out on his head. He wanted to rest
easy at night, and his horse farm in Oregon was not going
to happen if the Pinkertons rode close behind, dogging his
every step. The way to turn the Pinkertons into allies was

to capture the real robbers and see to it they got the credit—or any reward.

"Attempted robbers," Slocum said disdainfully. He had robbed a stage or two in his day. Nothing he was proud of, but he had done a good job of it, unlike the four or five highwaymen after this stagecoach. They had been driven off too easily, considering the firepower turned against them from the coach. The guard and passengers would have run out of ammunition fast if the robbers had launched a real attack, but they had been too cowardly.

Or was there something Slocum was missing?

He followed the tracks down to a riverbank where they vanished in the water. Looking around, he decided the robbers would head downstream. Less than ten minutes later he found where they left the river and climbed the far bank, on foot and leading their horses. Slocum counted carefully now. Five sets of tracks, including the two distinctive ones. He was not sure where the fifth man had joined them. In the river? It did not matter. Slocum knew what he faced now.

The day passed slowly as he kept on their trail, intent on the spoor and looking for any possible trap ahead. The robbers were too confident of their escape, which bothered him. They might not have known the posse of Pinkerton detectives had been so close, but this worried Slocum, too. The robbers showed nothing but arrogance in their retreat from the stagecoach attack.

A gunshot brought Slocum up short. His hand flashed to his six-shooter, then he relaxed. The sound echoed through the forest from at least a mile off. The trees muffled it and robbed it of full resonance, but Slocum still homed in on the sound. He tethered his sorrel and advanced through the forest until he heard angry voices.

"That's all? We busted our butts and one damned bag of coins is all we got?"

Slocum moved like a shadow until he got closer to the

five robbers. They stood around a strongbox. One had shot the lock off. This had been the sound Slocum had heard. The man bounced a heavy leather bag in his palm.

"We got plenty and for no risk," the one Slocum pegged as leader said. "There must be a hundred dollars in here."

"That's only ten dollars apiece," complained another of the robbers. "I kin work and make more 'n that in a day, and without the risk of gettin' my fool head shot off."

Slocum wondered at the poor arithmetic showed by the robber. But none of the others called him on it. They were either stupid or the gold was divvied up in a some way other than even-steven. Slocum knew, among men like this, greed outweighed stupidity. They would painfully divide the gold one coin at a time until each had an equal share, if that had been the original agreement.

Half the gold went somewhere else. To five others?

"We kin take off and not look back. We kin double our take if—"

"Don't even think on it, Potter," the leader said coldly. "We don't dare double-cross them."

"Why? Will they sic the Pinkertons on us?" Potter said sarcastically.

"It's not worth an extra ten dollars apiece," the leader said, standing. He kicked at the strongbox. "We got to talk with them because they said there'd be more in the box."

"Let's get out of here," Potter said.

Slocum watched the road agents leave. He waited ten minutes before slipping from his hiding place and going to the rifled strongbox. As they had said, the solitary bag of coins was the only thing of value inside. Or was it?

Slocum rummaged in the bottom of the box and pulled out several envelopes stuffed with documents. He saw these had been sealed and carried various names on the fronts. Gold was valuable enough to be shipped in a strongbox, but papers? What were these? Slocum was not sure, so he stuffed them into his shirt. Returning them to the Santa Rosa sheriff would go a ways toward proving he had nothing to do with the robbery.

Now all he had to do was catch the five highwaymen and retrieve the gold they had stolen.

Slocum snorted and shook his head.

"All I have to do," he said softly, wondering how he was going to do it.

Slocum slept fitfully, finally coming awake an hour before dawn. He took a deep breath, stretched his sore, cramped muscles, and then knew he had to act soon. Following the gang got him nowhere. If he found their hideout, he had to tell the Santa Rosa sheriff or the head of the Pinkerton detectives. Neither seemed a good choice if they thought he was part of the gang.

Hitching up his gun belt, Slocum moved silently through the cold forest. His boots crushed pine needles and dried leaves, but the soft crunching sound was masked by the wind whistling through the treetops. He got back to the campsite and looked it over again. The two men supposedly guarding the camp were asleep, almost where they had been before. The others snored peacefully. After this much sleep, they would be groggy and slow to act when they got up.

Slocum intended to be sure that happened on his terms.

He edged around until he was directly behind one sleeping sentry. His Colt Navy slid from its holster with a soft hiss, then flashed through the air to buffalo the guard. The man slumped to the side, unconscious.

"So far, so good," Slocum said to himself, moving to the next guard. This one fell as easily as the first because he had been sitting up, his head exposed. The other three lay under their blankets and would be harder to cold-cock.

Walking carefully through the camp, Slocum stopped

beside one sleeping figure and judged how best to continue. He dropped to one knee, got his bearings, then
acted. One hand clamped firmly on the man's mouth to
keep him from crying out as his other pinched shut the
prominent Roman nose poking up from the blankets. The
man thrashed about but, caught by surprise and still
asleep, he passed out without making too much noise.

Slocum could throw down on the other two, wake them
and then tie them up, but he preferred all five to be unconscious. It made handling the sidewinders that much
easier. He started to repeat the move of pinching off the
air on the next man—Potter—when he realized he had
reached down and grabbed a toe rather than a nose.

Potter kicked out, knocking Slocum to the ground.

"What's going on? Hey, who the hell are you!" Potter
grabbed for his six-shooter, cocked and fired it while it
was still in the holster. A bit of flying leather hit Slocum
in the forehead and knocked him back down while the
more dangerous bullet whined off into the night.

"Why'd you shoot?" demanded the gang leader, sitting
upright. He grabbed for his rifle when he spotted the intruder, and Slocum knew hell was out for lunch. From
the awkward sitting position he could not get to his six-
shooter in its cross-draw holster so he rolled and came up
to hands and knees.

"A sneak thief!" cried Potter. "He tried to rob me in
my sleep!"

Lead flew everywhere now. Slocum dropped to his
belly and let both men fill the air above him with bullets,
then scuttled off for the cover afforded by the forest. He
had come close to snaring all five but had made a bad
mistake when it mattered most.

"What's wrong with you varmints?" Potter screamed.
"Shoot him!"

"They're knocked out," the gang leader called. "He got
them first. He must be the law!"

This caused a new leaden barrage to come into the forest seeking Slocum's hide. He crouched behind a tree and heard bullets thudding into the wood at his back. Knowing that he had missed a golden opportunity, he dashed deeper into the woods.

Whatever he did now wasn't going to include the capture of the five men. How he could square himself with the Pinkertons was a mystery he would have to work out. Then Slocum realized he had bigger troubles brewing.

Potter came after him, the leader following. From the sound of their footsteps on the dried leaves, a third member of the gang joined them. It wouldn't be long before the other two were back in action and fighting mad. No one likes being made a fool of, and Slocum had done a right fine job of that knocking them out while they slept on guard duty.

"Be real careful, Ned," Potter called to the gang leader. "We seen one of them, but marshals travel with posses."

"Gus!" Slocum called. "Get the rest of the Pinkertons circling 'round them!" He hoped to spook Ned and Potter and make them wary of coming after him. Convincing the law he had nothing to do with the stagecoach holdup was one thing, getting away from the robbers without taking a few bullets was another—and it was paramount in his head right now.

To Slocum's surprise, the robbers laughed. He went cold inside. That told him where some of the loot from the holdup was going. The Pinkerton leader had latched onto Slocum as a scapegoat and had been in on the robbery from the beginning.

Something else worried at Slocum until it all fell into place. When he had ridden up, the driver, guard, and passengers had been putting up a vigorous fight. The highwaymen were riding around the stranded stagecoach, circling in like vultures to take their prize. The only problem was that they *had* stolen the strongbox. When? The shooting had to be for show to convince the passengers the fight was for real. Either the driver or shotgun messenger had already thrown the strongbox out for the robbers. The rest had been a charade.

The man leading the Pinkerton posse, the driver, and the guard made three more in on the robbery. Were there two more or had the mastermind demanded a double share? They had gone to incredible trouble for ten dollars each in gold.

And it made Slocum's plan to catch the gang and turn them over to the Pinkertons worthless. Gus would never listen, insisting to his superintendent that Slocum was the real robber. If Slocum wanted out from under the false charges, he had to go either to the Santa Rosa sheriff or hightail it out of the countryside.

"Do that and the Pinkertons will follow me to the ends of the earth," Slocum grumbled. He was caught between a rock and a hard spot. Trusting the unknown sheriff felt like a new way of committing suicide to him, but what else could he do?

He touched the packets of paper he had rescued from the opened strongbox. They might get him a moment's notice and keep him out of jail long enough to make his case.

If he survived the next few minutes. He heard the gang fanning out as they stalked him. Slocum had a full cylinder in his Colt and now regretted not shooting the stagecoach robbers where they laid. If he had killed them in cold-blood, he wouldn't be worried about his own neck right now.

Making a lot of noise, Slocum ran directly away from the robbers. When he was sure they heard and followed, he used every Indian trick he had ever learned or heard of to silently climb a tree without rustling its leaves or leaving a trail up the bark to betray his passage. He laid flat on his belly along the overhanging limb of an oak and waited for the gang to walk under him.

Five minutes passed and Slocum worried they had lost his trail. That left them out combing the woods and shooting wildly at anything that moved. They might take out one another, but Slocum could not count on all five getting ventilated. Then he worried that they had not lost his trail and had seen through his ruse.

From all directions came deliberate footsteps. He heard harsh breathing and grunts as the outlaws stumbled through the dark while they converged on the tree where he hid.

His retreat was blocked. They had circled him and had him boxed in. Slocum gripped his Colt Navy harder and prepared for the fight of his life.

8

Slocum held his breath and waited for the shooting to start. He wanted to kill as many of the outlaws as he could before they got him. Lungs straining and beginning to burn, he let out his breath slowly and wondered where the robbers had gone. There had been no mistaking the way they had been creeping up around him like a ring of wolves after a sheep. Slocum wished he could push aside the thick oak leaves and peer down at the ground to see what was going on, but any rustling in the branches would give away his position.

Canting his head to one side, Slocum strained to hear the slightest sound below him. An early rising squirrel ran along a thick limb above him and jumped gracefully to another tree. A faint breeze stirred the leaves and animals began moving in the forest, but Slocum had heard the gang coming toward him from every direction and did not hear them now. That meant they laid in wait for him to come down. He knew it in his bones.

Slocum holstered his six-shooter, stood without making too much commotion among the thick leaves and then edged toward the sturdy oak trunk. He made more noise than he liked as he climbed to the branch recently vacated by the agile gray squirrel. From this lofty point, Slocum could see some of the ground around him.

His gut instincts had been right. Two highwaymen aimed their rifles at the base of the tree where he had sought refuge, waiting to plug him the instant he showed himself. He didn't have to look around to know the other three were similarly arrayed and ready to shoot. Slocum considered his chance of killing both the outlaws he had spotted, then decided against such foolhardy gunplay. At one point, he had been three up on the gang and had still lost. With all of them ready, taking out two only meant the other three had a better chance of shooting him.

Slocum climbed slowly, still trying to move as quietly as possible. To his ears he might as well have had a brass band hammering out a tune to draw attention, but the outlaws never looked up. He knew they would get itchy trigger fingers soon and come looking for him. He wanted to be far gone when that happened.

The next branch up was flimsier, but Slocum dared to go to the far end. Directly below him he saw the gang's leader. Ned carried two six-guns, one in each hand, and looked as if he might be able to use them. All the grim-faced robber had to do was look up and he would have an easy target.

Slocum kept inching along the increasingly shaky limb until one from an adjacent tree poked him in the ribs. Transferring his grip, Slocum pulled himself along the other tree's branch until he reached that trunk. He was now outside the ring of death girdling the other tree, but that didn't mean he was in the clear.

Making his way like the squirrel that had preceded him on this aerial route, he jumped to the next tree and the one beyond it before skinning down to the ground. From this vantage he could see only one outlaw, and the road agent was getting antsy. The man waved frantically to

Ned, who rose slightly and motioned him back into hiding.

Slocum knew their patience would give out soon. He made his way through the forest, walking faster as dawn filtered down past the tall trees, until he reached his sorrel. The animal neighed. Slocum quickly calmed the horse, then mounted, and rode away quietly until he had gone a quarter mile. Then he put his heels into the mare's flanks and galloped away from the deadly trap behind him.

When the horse began to tire, Slocum slowed the pace and took time to think through his predicament. Intruding on the stagecoach robbery had been bad luck on his part and he ought to have joined in fighting the gang right away. Having the passengers on his side might have counted for something. Or maybe not, if the driver and shotgun messenger were in cahoots with the gang.

"The gang and the head of the Pinkerton posse," he said in disgust. Leaving the entire mess behind him was the best solution except for the Pinkertons. Allan Pinkerton had built his reputation on never letting any criminal escape his clutches and had instilled this in all his field operators. Slocum had met more than one in his day and dogged determination was the single trait they all shared. They might be smart or dumb, quick or slow, but they were all filled with persistence.

If they lacked this focus, the higher-ups at Pinkerton National Detective Agency headquarters back in New York City got rid of them fast. Gossip had it that even Pinkerton's son took part in tracking down wanted criminals. The agency wanted their posters circulated faster than federal or state posters and usually carried higher rewards.

Slocum might outrun a federal warrant for killing a judge but he couldn't escape the Pinkerton wanted poster, should Gus post it. And Slocum knew he would because of the way Ned and the rest had acted when he had tried to decoy them. Gus was in on the robberies. The Pinkerton agent might get the information about the shipments or find out from the driver and stagecoach guard. However it worked, Gus was in the robbery up to his eyeballs.

Fumbling around inside his shirt, Slocum pulled out the thick envelopes that had been in the strongbox. Opening them might give a clue where safety lay, but he knew better than to disturb the seals. Returning them intact gave him his best chance of throwing Gus, Ned, and the rest behind bars.

As much as he hated the notion, he had to rely on the Santa Rosa sheriff being honest. There was nowhere else to turn. Slocum got his bearings from the rising sun, then headed for Santa Rosa and what might be his own necktie party.

The sun was sinking in the west by the time Slocum rode into town. Santa Rosa was like so many others in California. It had been a boom town during gold rush days and then had faded in glory and population when the gold petered out. What kept it going now seemed to be logging, along with some hydro-mining in a gulch he passed on his way.

The heavy hydraulic hoses blasted waist-thick torrents of water into the ground and gnawed away tons of the riverbank to carry the sludge down to rockers that sifted out the gold or whatever mineral the miners sought to pull from the ground. It left behind unsightly debris and about the ugliest cutbanks Slocum had ever seen.

This wasn't his concern. Clearing his name and not getting killed was.

As he rode down the main street in Santa Rosa Slocum marvelled at everything that had happened to him. He was leaving behind a wake of men willing to kill him for things he either never did or had done to save someone else. Ralston and Porges and Captain Greer, unknown killers in Oakland and now the stagecoach robbers and their allies all wanted him dead.

For all he knew, Michael Porges might, too. Slocum had no idea if the young man blamed him for getting shot. He certainly had to fault Slocum for returning him to his father's clutches where his stepmother could rip him to bloody ribbons verbally, if not physically.

Slocum licked his lips as he peered into the Solitary Gent Saloon and Dance Hall. Boisterous laughter came from inside, mingled with feminine squeals of glee and the indescribable odor of spilled, stale beer. Slocum wanted a drink, needed one, but he rode past the saloon and went on to the town's jailhouse. He might be trading his freedom for a cell—or worse—but he had to try.

Easing his six-shooter out of his holster and then letting it slip back, he went into the sheriff's office. A gray-haired, scrawny man sat behind the battered oak desk. As he looked up, light from the coal oil lamp glinted off his badge.

"Sheriff?"

"That's me. What can I do for you?"

"Well, Sheriff, this is a twisted story and might take a few minutes."

"All I got ahead of me tonight is busting up fights over at the saloon and filling out papers to serve, something that pays me all right but is downright boring."

Slocum launched into his story, watching the old sheriff carefully for any sign the man might go for the six-gun at his side or grab for the shotgun leaning in the corner. After he dropped the papers on the desk, he edged back until the sheriff could reply.

The sheriff leafed through the envelopes, then looked up at Slocum.

"You ever hold up a stagecoach?" he asked bluntly.

"Now that would be a real dumb thing for me to confess to," Slocum said. "What I'm telling you is that I had nothing to do with holding up this one."

"This might surprise you, but I believe you, Slocum." The sheriff leaned back. Slocum watched to be sure he wasn't going for the scattergun. The sheriff locked his fingers behind his head and hiked his feet up to the desk. "I been real suspicious of Gus Potter for some time now."

"Potter? Does he have a brother?"

"Might. Why?"

"One of the gang's named Potter." ·

"That's real interesting. Now me and the Pinkerton superintendent for the district have locked horns over the men he sends out here. Last time I complained, he declared he'd keep his posse at home and make me suffer. When the current batch of detectives showed up a month back, I thought that was strange but didn't question it. The stage company seemed to welcome them."

"You think Gus Potter might not be a Pinkerton detective?"

"Playing one don't seem too hard to me. Might send a telegram to the main office down in San Francisco and check this out. Never cared much for Gus Potter from the day he came to town. And the driver and guard are real chummy with him, too."

Slocum said nothing. Let the lawman put the pieces together to suit himself. That made Slocum's case all the stronger.

"You say all they got was a small bag of gold?"

"They claimed it amounted to ten dollars apiece. That and the envelopes were all that was in the strongbox."

"Now that is passing strange since the stagecoach agent claimed to have lost danged near a thousand dollars in gold."

"Looks like you have a den of vipers in Santa Rosa, Sheriff."

"Don't it ever," the old man said. He fixed Slocum with

his steely stare, then dropped his feet from the desk and leaned forward. "You're going to help out while I sweep them all out, aren't you, Slocum?"

Slocum knew he had no choice.

"How many of them do you really trust, Sheriff?" Slocum asked, looking at the posse the lawman had assembled.

"Not a danged one of them, but they're better than the Pinkerton boys."

The sheriff had searched Santa Rosa from one end to the other hunting for Gus Potter and the rest of his Pinkertons. One by one he had found the men—all except Potter. Most were drunk or with whores. By the time he had herded them into the town jail, the telegram from San Francisco arrived giving the sheriff the information he had requested.

The superintendent of the San Francisco Pinkerton office had never assigned Gus Potter or any of the others to Santa Rosa. A careful reading of the wire convinced him that the Pinkerton super had never even heard of Gus Potter.

Slocum stared into the forest, in the direction of the outlaw camp he had left the day before. It struck him as absurd for the robbers to remain, but from the evidence, Ned and the other outlaws had not budged. Slocum decided they might not be the smartest crooks in the world from the way they acted.

That made them even more dangerous when they got cornered. They would fight with mindless fury.

"I got fifteen men working their way around the campsite, Slocum. If even one or two of them actually fires his six-shooter, we got 'em trapped like gophers."

"They might dig their way out," Slocum said. He worried that the greenhorns the sheriff had deputized might all turn tail and run at the first gunshot.

The sheriff laughed and slapped Slocum on the back.

"Old son, you worry too much. These gents are dumb as dirt."

Slocum wondered if he spoke of the robbers or his deputies. Then it stopped mattering. The distant crack of a six-gun brought him around. Slocum slid his Winchester from its sheath and looked to the sheriff for the command to advance. The sheriff waited until a half dozen more shots were fired, then put his fingers in his mouth and let out a shrill whistle, signaling his posse to attack.

The fight was short, fierce, bloody. Despite Slocum's misgivings, the old sheriff had recruited well. The posse rounded up the surviving outlaws and held them in the center of the camp.

"Now, isn't this a sight for sore eyes," the sheriff said, staring down at Ned's lifeless body. "Ned Volks. He's got a whacking big bounty on his head. How much is it? Ten dollars?"

The sheriff laughed, but Slocum was in poor humor; Gus Potter had been caught with the others and he looked daggers at Slocum. The man's brother had been killed, and he obviously blamed Slocum for the death.

"We even got the driver and guard. Who else was in on this, Gus?"

"Go to hell!" Potter shouted. "I'm a Pinkerton man and was here to arrest the gang."

"Heard back from San Francisco," the sheriff said, smiling wickedly, "and know you for the lyin' son of a bitch you are. How many have died in the past month? Four? Five? You got a powerful lot to be held accountable for."

Gus Potter spat at Slocum as he passed him.

"You made yourself a real enemy there, old son," the sheriff said. "Don't go worryin' your head none, though. The circuit judge is in town. We'll have them convicted before the sun sets again."

"Then I'll be on my way," Slocum said. Silence met

his simple statement. Then he locked eyes with the sheriff and knew it wasn't going to be that simple.

"Reckon I'd be a mite happier if you came back to Santa Rosa with us to testify. Fact is, you're about the best witness I have against them."

"I make a terrible witness," Slocum said.

"Do your best, old son, do your best." The sharpness in the old man's voice told Slocum he had no choice. "Or else."

Slocum didn't have to ask what the 'or else' might be. He did not want to share a cell with Gus Potter until the trial.

9

The sheriff had been right about the judge wanting to get the trial over in a hurry. The posse with Gus Potter and the surviving members of the gang in captivity had hardly arrived in Santa Rosa when court was convened.

"Go on, Slocum," urged the sheriff, as they entered the Solitary Gent Saloon. "Say your piece so's we can get this over." The sheriff herded him toward the bar like a calf to a branding.

Slocum was sworn in, hand on a tattered Bible with more than half the pages missing, and then sat in a chair next to the bar where the judge presided. He was uncomfortable with the proceedings because he suspected the sheriff had not caught the entire gang. Gus Potter was guilty, as were the rest of the outlaws brought in for trial, but a piece was missing. If Slocum's testimony convicted the men in the docket and one gang member remained free, he would have to watch his back every second of the day and twice as hard all night.

He shrugged it off. He had to watch out now. He was racing through California, picking up enemies the way a dog picks up fleas. What was another man or two wanting to kill him?

"Tell us what happened," the judge said pompously. "In your own words."

"Can't use any other words but my own," Slocum allowed. He launched into a recitation of all that had happened. It took the better part of ten minutes until the judge motioned him to silence.

"That's good, Mr. Slocum. What was in them envelopes the varmints didn't steal?"

"They stole them, Your Honor." The sheriff spoke up. "They left them behind in the strongbox, preferring to take only the gold."

At that Slocum went cold inside. He remembered how the sheriff had mentioned the town's stagecoach agent reporting thousands of dollars in gold missing. If he had to put down a bet, his money was on the stage agent as being in the gang, also.

"What were they?" the judge asked. "The envelopes?"

"Legal papers, deeds, things of no importance to a thief but powerful necessary for the conduct of determining property rights, Your Honor."

"Grand theft, then. And murder. You varmints been shootin' up the stage for the past month. And you lied 'bout being Pinkerton agents. I could send you back to San Francisco and let the Pinkerton Agency superintendent deal with you, but I won't."

Slocum saw relief on the men's faces. Then they all turned pale when the judge continued.

"For killin' five good and true men over the past month, I sentence you all to hang. Right now. No reason to put off doin' what has to be done."

"You can't do that!" shouted Gus Potter. "There's no evidence against us for those killings. We robbed the stage. I admit that, but we didn't get squat! The strongbox was empty!"

"Stupid *and* murderous swine," the judge intoned. "Go

on, get them out and hang them. That cottonwood down the road ought to do just fine, Sheriff."

"No!" Gus Potter tried to get away, but the men in the sheriff's posse swarmed him and knocked him to the saloon floor.

"Your Honor," Slocum spoke up. "The sheriff mentioned to me that the stagecoach agent reported a whale of a lot more money having been taken during this robbery."

"So? He was wrong."

"What if he took the gold for himself, knowing the stage was going to be robbed?"

"You callin' George Stuart a thief? Why, he's related to Jeb Stuart himself. A finer man never lived."

"I'm related to General Stuart, too!" shouted Gus Potter from the bottom of the pile of struggling deputies.

Slocum looked at the sheriff, wondering if the lawman understood what Potter was saying. He seemed to.

"You mean you and George Stuart are related?"

"He's my uncle. My mother's brother!" shouted Potter. "I can't believe he double-crossed us like this!"

Slocum edged for the door and slipped out into the night. Santa Rosa was deserted, all the action focused on the courtroom drama in the saloon. He wasted no time getting to his horse and riding from town. He had condemned a man whose uncle was still on the loose, a man who had shown he was capable of double-dealing and maybe murder.

He doubted Stuart had abandoned his nephew. More likely, Gus Potter and George Stuart—and Gus's dead brother—were going to split the take and deal the rest of the gang out. Blood was thicker than water, especially among thieves. Since Slocum's testimony knotted the noose around Potter's neck, that meant Stuart was likely to be out for revenge.

"Why the hell not?" Slocum grumbled. If he got

enough men mad at him, they might take to killing one another for the pleasure of shooting him.

Slocum rode hard and fast to put as many miles between him and Santa Rosa as he could, heading toward the Pacific coast since the inland road was turning too dangerous to continue traveling. It hardly seemed like enough distance had been covered when the sorrel began to tire and he decided to rest for the night. Not enough by half.

The coastal range rose and fell and cast its shadow on Slocum's back as he finally reached the coast. The sun had come up three hours earlier, giving Slocum a fine view of the uneasy Pacific with its whitecaps and rolling waves crashing tirelessly against the coast. He was not exactly sure where he had come out but thought Bodega Bay was a mile or two north.

As he rode slowly, he stared at the line where ocean met sky. Slocum shuddered. If he had not had the foresight to carry the dynamite when he had gone after Michael Porges, he might be on a clipper ship somewhere beyond that horizon. He wished he had a few sticks riding in his saddlebags right now. With the life he lived, Slocum never knew when he might need a bang a bit bigger than that afforded by his six-shooter or rifle.

The ground turned rockier and then he found a deeply rutted road leading into the town of Bodega Bay. The seabirds squawked endlessly and circled over his head like white vultures. The small town nestled along the curving bay where it met the Pacific looked to be a prosperous stopover for the ships plying their way up and down the coast between San Francisco and Seattle. Fishing boats came and went from the sheltered harbor, and Slocum spotted dozens of shark fins cutting silently through the water.

As he made his way down from the road toward the

town located on the northern shore of the bay, he saw two larger ships off the coast, waiting for the evening tide to come in. Bodega Bay was definitely a prosperous town, unlike so many of the ghost towns inland abandoned after the Gold Rush.

After all he had been through the past few days, Slocum wanted to spend a few days eating decent meals and sleeping in a soft bed. He found a small inn near the harbor.

"You don't have the look of a seaman," the proprietor said, a gimlet eye fixed on him.

"I need a stable for my horse," Slocum said. "I'll stay a day or two and then move on, but I want the sorrel to get some grain and a good rest."

"Been on the trail long?"

"Too long, it seems sometimes," Slocum answered. "There some place in town you'd recommend for dinner?"

"Down by the docks is a decent place, if you like fish. My sister runs it," the man explained. "The Flying Dutchman, she calls it. And if you leave your horse, I'll get it down to my brother-in-law. He runs the only livery in town."

"Thanks," Slocum said. He left the small inn and stepped into the cold evening. It felt good not to look over his shoulder constantly. As he rode over the mountains he had felt George Stuart's hot breath on his neck the entire way. Worst of all, he had no idea what Stuart even looked like, but that didn't keep Slocum from dreading meeting up with him. By now his nephew was dangling from a tree with his neck stretched and his other nephew dead from the sheriff's bullets.

Thankfully, Slocum had seen no one on the road to Bodega Bay.

He ducked into the restaurant recommended by the innkeeper and sat down so he could look out a small window on the bay. Slocum ate slowly and enjoyed every bite of the sea bass, with all the trimmings. He usually preferred a good steak, but the lighter fare went down well and settled just fine in his belly after all the cans of beans and peaches he had eaten on the trail.

"Want anything else, mister?" asked the young man serving him. "Don't want to rush you but we got a ship haulin' mail up the coast comin' into port tonight. Them sailors get mighty hungry."

"Nothing else," Slocum said, pushing back from the table. If he stayed here too long, he'd get fat. The food was good, and he told the young man this.

"Thanks, mister. That's my mother doin' the cooking," he said proudly.

Slocum stepped back into the windy evening and saw the waiter had been right. A three-masted ship had come into port on the tide. Through the darkness Slocum saw two longboats rowing for the shore. The ship had not come directly to dock, probably because the harbor wasn't deep enough for such a large ship. He frowned as he studied the ship, wondering what might be wrong with it. Tossed on the waves, the ship seemed to list to one side, as if it was taking water.

He shrugged it off. He had no real interest in ships or sailing. A good piece of ocean fish every few years suited him just fine. Slocum walked along the road in front of the restaurant, looking for something to do. Any port city had more than one saloon, and he found one easily enough, brightly lit with boisterous laughter coming from inside.

Slocum stood in the doorway, looking over the place. The sailors who had not already passed out drunk worked diligently toward that end. Nothing to interest him, he decided. A poker game would be good, although he did not need the money at the moment. As he turned to go, he bumped into a burly sailor coming in from the street.

"Sorry," Slocum said. He looked curiously at the salt, who recoiled and then jumped as if someone had stuck him with a needle. The sailor backed off, then set off running.

Slocum shook his head in wonder. It had been a spell since he had frightened anyone so severely, and he had not even tried. Slocum got a few steps, then paused, staring back into Bodega Bay. Another clipper ship sailed into port, barely making the tide. It dropped anchor not far from the first vessel.

Frowning, Slocum again wondered what was wrong with the already-anchored clipper ship. It leaned even more precariously to one side as the waves lifted and dropped it.

"Looks like somebody blew the side out of it," Slocum said. He started to laugh. Then his belly tightly knotted. Memory returned in a flash. The sailor who had run off had been on Captain Greer's ship. Slocum squinted a little as he studied the damaged ship in the harbor. He had not gotten a good enough look at Greer's ship back in San Francisco before he blew a hole in the side, but this one might be its twin.

It might even be Greer's ship. Slocum had no idea how it could have been salvaged, but he had not seen it go to the bottom. He had only seen it sinking. A good captain might have saved his vessel.

"Greer," Slocum grated out, seeing the sailor he had bumped into coming back with four other seamen—and the angry Captain Greer. The captain banged a short, ugly-looking club against one palm as he walked, waiting to replace his calloused hand for Slocum's head.

Slocum took the leather thong off the hammer of his six-gun, then stepped back into dense shadows. He had no reason to shoot it out with the captain, as much as he disliked him and his shanghaiing ways. But if it came down to gunning down the captain or having him use that short, sturdy belaying pin on his head, Slocum knew which he would pick.

"Where'd that son of a barnacle go?" demanded the captain.

"He was comin' out of the saloon," the sailor said.

"He's not in there now," reported another sailor.

Slocum watched as they stood in a tight knot discussing what to do next. He didn't want to tangle with any of them. They were all heavier than he was and carried a respectable amount of spite for what he had done to their ship. Slocum would have been content to let the matter drop, but he saw Greer's face and knew that wouldn't happen.

The captain wanted revenge.

"He couldn't have gone far. Find him. And when you do, I want him. This is personal!"

Slocum sidled along in the shadows and found a narrow alley between buildings that took him to the next street away from the harbor. Proprietors were closing their stores, giving Slocum no place to hide. He started back for the inn and banged into the sailor who had originally spotted him.

"You, it's you, the one who scuttled our ship!" The sailor swung clumsily. Slocum easily ducked the punch but knew he wasn't going to be this lucky if the others joined the fight.

"You got me confused with someone else," Slocum said, playing for time.

"It's you. I'd know you anywhere." The sailor squared his stance and got ready for a round of fisticuffs Slocum doubted would last too long. The sailor was bigger, stronger, and had his land legs back.

"Is that Greer?" Slocum asked, looking past the sailor's shoulder. The man hesitated a brief instant, turning his head slightly in the direction glanced. This was all the opening Slocum needed to swing a haymaker that landed in the middle of the sailor's gut. Slocum felt the shock of his hard fist hitting equally hard muscled belly, but the blow was enough to fold the sailor like a bad poker hand.

Slocum grabbed the unconscious man's collar and dragged him down the street until he came to another deserted alley. Tearing strips from the man's own shirt, Slocum bound his hands behind his back, then stuffed him into a rain barrel. He found the lid and pounded it down firmly, sealing the sailor inside.

"One down, five to go," Slocum said. He wanted to avoid shooting the sailors. He didn't have a grudge to settle with them. If there was a score to even, it was with Greer.

He looked up and down the street and saw three of the seamen rounding the corner twenty yards away. Slocum jumped to the barrel where he had packed away the first sailor, then pulled himself to the roof of a boardinghouse. He watched the sailors storm past, cursing as they went. From what he could make of their cursing, Greer had offered a ten dollar reward and double rum rations to the man who caught Slocum.

Slocum felt annoyed at how little Greer was willing to pay for him. Walking carefully on the sloping roof, he went in the opposite direction from the trio of sailors. At the other side of the boardinghouse, Slocum paused a moment, then jumped to the roof of a bakery. The slick shingles under his boots betrayed him.

Sliding down, he thrashed about trying to stop his fall off the roof. Slocum grabbed wildly at the edge of the roof, only to have his fingers slip at the last instant. He landed heavily in the street.

Slocum looked up at Greer and the remaining sailor.

"Lookee what dropped into our laps, Captain," the sailor said.

The man was willing to waste time gloating. Slocum acted. He kicked out hard, his boot sole catching the sailor's kneecap. With a shriek of pain, the man fell, clutching his damaged knee. Slocum rolled fast. Greer barely missed crushing his skull to a bloody pulp with his belaying pin. Slocum kept rolling until he crashed into the side of the bakery.

"I'll kill you, you drowned rat," cried Greer. "You turned my ship into a worthless coastal hopper. There's no way I can ever repair the old *Neptune* so's to make it seaworthy again. All I kin do is move mail up and down the coast. Damned mail!"

"You shouldn't shanghai men," Slocum said, getting to his feet. He used both arms to block an overhead blow from the captain. The wood club cracked into his forearms and shocked him with the intense pain it caused.

"Every captain does that. I ought to keep you for my crew. It'd be good seeing you given twenty lashes now and then while you're eating nothing but hardtack and sleeping in the bilge."

Like his mate, Greer talked too much. Slocum gauged the distance and had plenty of time to judge what to do. His left arm was numb from the blow but his right was as good as gold when he drew his Colt Navy and shoved it hard into Greer's face.

The captain missed with his belaying pin and tried to avoid the six-shooter's muzzle. Slocum pulled the trigger. The bullet missed Greer's head but the muzzle was next to the sea captain's ear. The loud report deafened him and sent a dagger of sharp pain into his head.

This gave Slocum the chance to twist around and use his six-gun like a club. He hit Greer hard just over the ear he had just deafened. The captain fell heavily, groaning and weakly fighting. Slocum hit him again. This time Greer collapsed and did not move.

"You kilt him!" cried the sailor with the broken knee-cap. The man scuttled off like a crab searching for his shipmates. Slocum considered putting a bullet into the injured man to shut him up, then decided he didn't need to explain how he shot a crippled man in the back to the local marshal.

Slocum stood over Greer, his six-shooter pointed at the man's back. It would be better all around if he got rid of the captain once and for all. A single shot would do it. Slocum's finger tightened on the hair trigger, then eased off as a more fitting punishment came to him.

Grinning ear to ear, Slocum got his arms around Greer's body and dragged him off where he could work on the man a mite without being interrupted by the captain's crew.

It took Slocum almost ten minutes to strip off the uniform, leaving the captain dressed only in his longhandles. Tying and gagging the man, Slocum left him in an alley close to the saloon. Careful not to be spotted by the captain's crew, Slocum went into the saloon and looked over the crowd. He went directly to a officer at the end of the bar and spoke with him for several minutes, haggling over price.

"If he's as good as you say, I'll go ten dollars," the man said.

"Out back," Slocum said, leading the captain of the other clipper ship to where he had left Greer. The bound and gagged Greer stirred and began making muffled sounds. Slocum slugged him again.

"Careful, boyo, don't damage the merchandise." The other captain dropped to one knee and checked Greer's condition. "Looks as if he's spent a bit of time on the sea. Saves me havin' to train him all proper, though he is old."

"Not that old." Slocum enjoyed dickering over the price and finally got an extra two dollars.

"You want to help get him down to the longboat?" asked the captain who had just shanghaied Greer.

"All yours," Slocum said, resting his hand on the ebony butt of his six-shooter. He didn't want to end up on the same ship as Greer.

"Thank you for this fine specimen. Next time we're in port, if you got more, Captain Longbow'll be buyin'!"

"Have a safe trip," Slocum said as the captain dragged Greer off. "A safe, *long* trip."

As soon as Longbow was out of sight, Slocum returned to the inn, packed his gear and fetched his sorrel from the livery stables. Spending a night on a soft mattress would have been nice. Getting caught by Greer's men would not be so nice.

He rode ten miles in the dark, putting Bodega Bay behind him, before he stopped, tethered his horse, and spread his bedroll on the hard ground. Slocum slept the sleep of the righteous, content at the retribution he had delivered to Captain Greer.

10

Slocum rode along, chuckling to himself about how he had turned the tables on Greer. The shanghaiing captain deserved his fate. Slocum wasn't sure if Longbow would recognize Greer and let him go or if Greer's pleas would fall on deaf ears. If Longbow felt too threatened by his new crew member, he was likely to chuck Greer overboard in the middle of the ocean.

"Good riddance," Slocum said, smiling. He could not shanghai everyone gunning for him, but he felt Greer was gone for good, one way or the other. And Ralston was long behind him in San Francisco. The banker would have moved on to other grudges, sought other schemes to recoup his losses, found other men to hate.

With Ralston came thoughts of Michael Porges, Nathan Porges, Amelia Porges—and Julia.

Especially Julia. Slocum missed her, but it wasn't quite a longing for her warmth next to him in bed as it was curiosity about how she had done with her father and stepmother. Not that he would have kicked her out if he had found her curled up next to him. The send-off she had given him from San Francisco would be a cherished memory for quite a while, but Slocum felt as if he had abandoned her in the middle of a difficult situation.

He finally decided she would be all right. She had brains and looks and even wealth, if her stepmother didn't steal it all first, to make a success of whatever she tried.

The heat of the northern California summer sun beat down on Slocum's face, first his leathery right cheek and then as the day wore on, pounded his left. He basked in the sunlight like a lizard sunning itself, but as he rode he felt the hairs rising on the back of his neck.

He had gotten rid of Greer and outlegged the men in San Francisco gunning for him, but George Stuart remained at liberty. Somewhere. Would the stagecoach agent carry a grudge for all that had happened to his nephews? Slocum wished he had gotten a description of the man from the sheriff, but he hadn't. Now and again, Slocum glanced at his back trail hoping to catch sight of a rider.

It probably wouldn't be Stuart, but seeing another traveler would put his mind to rest. His sense of being watched would be vindicated. As it was, the longer he rode, the more troubled Slocum became. No one trailed him, but he felt down deep in his gut that someone did. He wasn't easily spooked and had learned to trust his instincts.

Evidence said he was alone, riding along the coast toward Point Arena. He had seen the light from the lighthouse the night before and had thought it only a day's ride off. He had misjudged the distance and was taking longer. Slocum looked around, then headed inland again, over the mountains toward Ukiah. He might lose whoever tracked him.

Or he might lose the sensation he was being followed by phantoms.

For three days he rode, wary of his back trail and for three days he had seen no one. Slocum heaved a sigh of relief when he saw the outskirts of Ukiah ahead. It was not much of a town but it had a railroad station and afforded him the chance of putting real miles behind him fast. Not even going to a restaurant for a meal, he made a beeline for the ticket office and bought a fare for himself and his horse going toward Yreka. After the two-day trip to the northern border of California, he could lose himself in the wilds of Oregon.

"You're in luck," the stationmaster said, pushing the ticket across the ledge to Slocum. "Train's due in any time now."

"I had wanted to get some grub," Slocum said, but his words were drowned out by the train whistle sounding the arrival. Steel screeched on steel and the train came to a halt in the station.

As hungry as he was, Slocum knew he could put to rest the uneasy feeling he had of being followed. He got his horse into a freight car, made sure the sorrel was secured, then returned to the platform and watched the passengers boarding.

They were the usual lot, as far as he could tell. Men with their wives, a tinker, two tinhorn gamblers who argued endlessly about the best ways to cheat at cards, a few farmers—but no one who looked as if he might shoot Slocum in the back.

He wondered what George Stuart looked like—any of these men, especially the ones traveling alone?

"Board, all aboard!" bellowed the conductor, swinging on a handrail at the side of the passenger car. Slocum still hesitated, waiting to see if there would be a last minute addition to the car.

The train began to spin its wheels and spit fat blue sparks. Slowly moving, it gathered power and speed. Only then did Slocum jump aboard and present his ticket to the conductor.

"You waitin' for someone?" the conductor asked. "I

seen you lookin' 'round like you missed 'im."

"Fellow name of George Stuart," Slocum said.

"Don't know him. Describe him. Maybe I seen him."

"That's all right," Slocum said, heaving a sigh of relief. He dropped into an empty seat, hiked up his feet, and tipped his hat down over his eyes to catch a few winks. For the first time since leaving Santa Rosa he relaxed. The rocking train lulled him to sleep.

Until a lurch threw him off the seat and onto the floor. Slocum grabbed for his six-shooter but was too twisted around to get it out. Then he settled down. Nothing had happened to him that had not also happened to the other passengers. Men cursed and women muttered under their breaths, trying to remain ladylike in the face of such a sudden stop.

Slocum got to his feet and lurched through the car. To his surprise the sun was low in the west. He had slept longer than anticipated. By now the train must have gone sixty miles or more, far beyond the ability of any man to ride in one day, even switching off periodically between two horses.

"What happened?" Slocum asked the conductor. The man looked irritated rather than frightened.

"It's not a holdup, if that's worrying you, mister," the conductor said. "There's a rail loose ahead and the engineer wanted to ease across it so we wouldn't derail."

"How's he know it's loose?"

The conductor snorted derisively. "We been over this route twice a week for the past year. Old Scanlon knows every rivet and tie like the back of his own hand."

"We're not moving," Slocum pointed out.

"Don't go readin' anything into that. We'll be on our way soon enough," the conductor said, but his words carried no conviction. As he went back into the passenger car to soothe the others, he left Slocum alone on the platform between cars.

Slocum swung out and looked ahead. Both the engineer and the fireman stood beside the tracks, scratching their heads. Seeing the train wasn't going to roll on and leave him, Slocum dropped to the ground and walked forward. The engine belched steam and sparks from the stack twisted like drunk fireflies in the twilight.

"Anything I can do?" Slocum asked, seeing them doing nothing more than staring.

"We got a bit of a problem," the engineer said. "Rail's come loose. If I take the locomotive over it, the entire train might derail."

"Can you fix it?"

"We got some equipment, but I dunno," said the fireman. "I never done anything like this before. I say we wait till a crew comes out down after us to see what happened."

"I don't like being so late," the engineer said. "They don't call me 'Stopwatch' for nuthin'."

"Stopwatch Scanlon?" Slocum asked.

"Do I know you? How'd you know my name?" the engineer asked.

"The conductor mentioned it. Look, I worked on a railroad for a spell out in Colorado and can help."

"Much obliged, mister," Scanlon said. Slocum and the engineer examined the rail, and it was as the man had said. The entire train would jump the track if they tried to roll over the rail in this condition.

The fireman fetched hammers and spikes from the caboose. With the conductor and most of the passengers looking on, Slocum and Scanlon began work on the rail until it got too dark to work.

"That won't hold, no sir," Scanlon said. "And it's too dark to work. We wait until first light and get back to the repairs."

"I want to go on tonight," Slocum said, the uneasy feeling returning now. A man with two horses could ride fifty miles a day, switching from one mount to the other as they tired. Any benefit he might have riding the train evaporated if they waited until the morning. Then Slocum shook his head. His imagination ran roughshod over his common sense. He had no evidence at all someone trailed him.

"Never mind," Slocum said quickly. "Morning will do."

He slept fitfully on the train, nightmares of dark-masked riders grabbing for him haunting his dreams.

"And I say, you should give him his fare back," Stop-watch Scanlon said, belligerently shoving out his chin. The conductor wasn't backing down.

"Nobody told him to help out. He done it of his own freewill."

"We'd still be out there if Slocum hadn't pitched in when he did," the engineer said. "Give him his damn fare back or I'll make you walk!"

Slocum stepped between the two arguing men and held up his hand. "That's all right. I don't need my money refunded. I was glad to help."

The jerkwater town where they had steamed in for water barely had three buildings other than the station. One of the buildings lacked a roof and the other two threatened to fall down if more than a puff of wind came by. It had taken a full day longer to reach the town than called for in the train schedule. The engineer was outraged at the delay and the conductor worried about money.

Slocum worried about ghosts on his trail.

"I'll give you a return ticket," the conductor said. "Good any time. Take it or leave it."

"That's fine," Slocum said. He spun when he heard footsteps behind him.

"You're mighty jumpy. The law's not after you, is it?"

asked the conductor. "Them's just more passengers gettin' on the train like they always do here."

Slocum studied the faces of the men climbing aboard and once more did not identify any of them. He wasn't sure what he expected. To see Ralston or Porges? He had no idea what George Stuart looked like. All the nervousness in the world wouldn't warn him about Stuart.

"It hasn't been the quickest trip, not like I expected," he said. The conductor took it personally, getting red in the face and then storming off. The engineer had already gone back to the cab and worked the valves to build up a head of steam. When the whistle screeched, Slocum got aboard and dropped into a seat again.

The conductor glared at him on his way to collect tickets from the new passengers. As he passed, Slocum grabbed his arm.

"Do you know them?" Slocum asked, jerking his thumb in the direction of the four men who had boarded at the water stop.

"Seen one or two of 'em before. They go to Yreka for supplies."

"But the other two?" pressed Slocum.

"I don't know them. Now give me back my arm, mister." The conductor finished his work as the train began lurching forward out of the station. Slocum was wary of the new passengers but none appeared dangerous.

But then would a stagecoach agent in Santa Rosa appear dangerous?

Slocum settled down again, letting the rolling motion of the train as it took the curves through the mountains soothe him until he drifted off to sleep again.

Slocum was doomed not to get a complete rest. He awoke to the sound of footsteps directly over his head. It took him a few seconds to realize what was going on. The train had slowed on a steep uphill grade and came perilously close to the inner embankment. Shrubs and even tree limbs brushed across the roof of the car. But it was not a tree branch that had awakened him.

The methodical step-step-step over his head was caused by a man walking on the roof. Slocum even imagined he heard spurs jingling as the man went from the middle of the car directly over Slocum to the back. When a second thud! in about the same spot echoed through the car, Slocum sat up and looked around.

The rest of the passengers either slept or talked with their traveling companions and had not noticed the curious sounds on the car roof. He eased the thong off the hammer of his Colt Navy and settled down to wait for what he knew had to follow. He switched seats so he had his back to the front wall of the passenger car and could see the others toward the rear.

Slocum saw nothing unusual in the passengers. None appeared nervous or expecting company. When the robber burst in through the rear door, the others jumped in surprise. None of them made a move to go for a six-shooter or to aid the train robber.

"This is a stickup!" the masked man barked. "Get your valuables out and drop 'em into this here barley sack." He held out a burlap gunnysack with one hand and waved a six-gun around with the other.

Slocum had too much money in his pocket to hand it over to any petty thief. He bided his time until the man was distracted, then stood, whipped out his Colt Navy and fired.

The round caught the robber in the shoulder. He screeched like a hoot owl, stumbled back, and sat down hard.

"Drop the gun or the next shot will be through your heart," Slocum ordered.

The startled robber did as Slocum told him. He tossed his six-shooter into the narrow aisle and tried to hold up his arms. His injured shoulder kept him from lifting his right arm higher than a few inches.

"Don't kill me, mister. You winged me. I'm trying to—"

Slocum remembered the second set of footsteps on the roof. The robber had a partner. He threw himself to one side as a shotgun blast ripped through the space where his head had been only a fraction of a second earlier.

Slocum hit the top of a seat—hard. His earlier wound along his rib stung like it had been dipped in liquid fire. He bounced off the seat, twisted around and fired at the second robber who had entered the car behind him.

If Slocum had not been ready for them, their robbery might have succeeded. One robbed the passengers starting at the rear of the car while the other stood guard at the front. They had jumped from an embankment and would have left the same way. The engineer and maybe the conductor would never have known there was any trouble on the train until later.

The men could have made a clean escape. If it hadn't been for Slocum.

He fired and fired again at the robber with the shotgun. The second bullet in the man's chest did not kill him. The third did. He sagged bonelessly to the floor, and his shotgun clattered loudly onto the platform between cars.

"You kilt him, you kilt my brother!" shouted the wounded robber still sitting in the aisle at the rear of the car.

Slocum said nothing. If he didn't shoot again, he might find yet another killer with a yen for his blood on his trail. He lifted his six-shooter and aimed at the screaming robber.

11

A thousand thoughts ran through Slocum's head. He had left too many men thinking about blood feuds behind him. Ralston thought he deserved money he had lost in a legitimate poker game. Nathan Porges was prodded by his wife into threatening Slocum's life because of the turmoil over who got the biggest slice of the family fortune. Slocum was sure Greer would gut him like a fish if he ever had the chance. And a man named Stuart might be willing to slit Slocum's throat because of his role in killing and hanging his relatives.

If Slocum let this train robber live, he stood the chance of having yet another man after his scalp. Slocum had drilled the other robber through the heart, and there was no doubt he was dead. The one in front of Slocum's Colt Navy might be a brother like he claimed or a cousin or just a partner. A partner might be more likely to declare vengeance on Slocum than a blood relative. All he had to do was pull the trigger and remove the threat.

"Stop!" shouted the conductor, stumbling into the car. He grabbed a cord and pulled hard on it, signaling the engineer to make an emergency stop. "You can't gun him down like this."

"He would have killed everyone on the train," Slocum said, still wrestling with the problem of killing the robber or trusting to the law to keep him locked up.

"There's no call for you to take the law into your hands. Put the damn gun down."

Slocum lowered his six-shooter a mite and saw the robber grabbing for his. Without thinking, Slocum aimed and fired. This time he shot the robber smack in the middle of the chest. The man died instantly.

"You went ahead and killed him after I told you not to!" raged the conductor.

"He was going for his gun," Slocum said. "Maybe you'd have liked it more if I let him shoot you or a couple passengers?"

"Off!" raged the conductor. "Get off my train!"

"What? We're in the middle of nowhere!"

"Get the hell off!"

Slocum saw the shocked expressions on the passengers' faces and shook his head in dismay. He had saved their lives and yet they sided with the conductor. Slocum stepped over the body of the robber he had just shot, made his way to the freight car and barely got his horse off before the train started rolling again. He soothed his horse and then started walking slowly parallel to the railroad tracks. The hum and rattle of steel on steel faded as the train left him farther behind.

In a way, Slocum was relieved. Having too many people around him made him uneasy. Being in the woods, the scent of redwood and pine in his nostrils, the soft familiar sounds of animals moving on their way, soothed him and assured him everything was all right. He did not have to look over his shoulder to simply travel.

He considered changing his direction of travel. East would get him over the Sierra Nevada mountains into territory he had not seen in months and months. But north was as good, even if killers might be dogging his steps.

Slocum heaved a sigh and wondered if he was being too suspicious. He had no proof anyone chased him. Meeting Greer in Bodega Bay had been pure coincidence, and Slocum had to admit there was no evidence anyone else came after him, intending to shoot him in the back. Let Ralston and the others rot in San Francisco. He was free and headed for country in Oregon sure to quiet his nerves.

He rode for another hour before a distant sound gnawed at the fringes of his senses. Slocum reined back and looked around. The steep climb into the mountains had leveled off into decent pasture land. He spotted deer grazing and other animals moving through the surrounding shelter of the wooded area. Then he realized the steel rails hummed again.

"Another train," he said, sighing. He rode a few yards away from the railroad bed to keep his horse from getting too spooked. Slocum even considered chasing some of the deer into the forest but decided against it. The train would roar past and let him be. He hooked his right leg around the saddle horn and leaned forward, waiting for the train.

Less than five minutes later, the engine puffed into view, white steam clouds billowing from the smokestack. Slocum saw this train pulled only a single car and made the grade into the pasture with little strain. Someone rich was in a powerful hurry to get up the line.

The engineer peered out of the cab at him as the train went by, then yelled at his fireman and began pulling on levers and opening valves. His whistle screeched like a hooty owl as he vented steam and steel wheels reversed on the tracks, sending sparks high into the air.

The train ground to a halt less than fifty feet away, showing how desperate the engineer had been to stop the powerful, heavy engine with its lone luxury Pullman car.

Slocum sat and watched. The back door opened and someone he recognized instantly came onto the back platform. His heart raced for a moment, then a sense of foreboding settled on him.

"John, John! I'm so glad I found you!"

He slid his leg back off the horse's back and got his right foot back into the stirrups. Slocum rode slowly to where he could tip his hat and greet Julia Porges.

"You're about the last person I thought to find out here," he said.

"John," the lovely woman said breathlessly, "I hoped against hope I'd find you! It's Michael."

"What about him? I haven't seen him."

"Then you know he ran off again?"

"Can't say that's so, but it wasn't much of a guess. If Michael lit out once, he'd keep doing it until he succeeded."

"It's Amelia. She drove him off. She was utterly horrible to him."

Slocum said nothing. Any man who couldn't stand up for himself, against his stepmother or even against his own father, wasn't much of a man. But then Julia seemed to have inherited the *cojones* in the Porges family.

"Help me, John. I know he's around here. I got a telegram from one of Papa's agents."

"Railroad agent? This is your father's line?"

"Why, yes, I thought you knew. Isn't that why you chose to go north?" She frowned. "Why are you on horseback? Your train is far ahead of this special."

"I got thrown off," Slocum said, not bothering to elaborate.

"It's my good luck, then. You can help me convince him to return to San Francisco."

"Why don't you let him go, Julia? He's not happy. Let Michael find his own way."

"I . . . I can't, John. If he goes, Amelia wins."

"Let her have the money. For all that, join Michael. The two of you can make it without your pa's pile of money. You're smart and pretty and can succeed wherever you are—without the Porges fortune."

Slocum wondered if something more than greed drove Julia when he saw the expression on her face. She fought to agree with him, but she didn't. She couldn't.

"Where is Michael?" Slocum asked, giving in to the inevitable.

"You really haven't seen him?"

"Of course not," Slocum replied. "I've been too busy staying alive."

"And getting thrown off Papa's trains," Julia said, grinning. Slocum had to laugh with her.

"That, too," he said. "You came this far north, so you must think he's around here somewhere."

"A small town along the line not five miles from here," Julia said. "Do help me, John. Please."

"All right," Slocum said. "Tell me what you know and how you know it." Slocum's suspicions soared again. He knew Amelia Porges was liable to plant false clues to her stepson's destination if it meant getting Julia out of her hair for a while. The more time Amelia spent with her husband, the deeper she sank her meat hooks into his fortune.

"A friend of mine works routing the engines. He is very good at it. Michael went to him and asked for the trains going to Cloverdale. But he never bought a ticket or used his pass."

"You think he hid on a freight car and got out of San Francisco without alerting anyone?"

"Yes," Julia said, her breasts rising and falling as her excitement mounted. "He tried to get away without anyone knowing."

"Couldn't he just read a schedule and not ask your friend?" Slocum asked. "Is Michael too stupid that he'd leave a trail you could follow so easily?"

"You mean *I* could follow?" Julia said, getting angry.

A flush came to her cheeks and highlighted the fine bones and her brown eyes. It made her even lovelier.

"That might be just what I mean," Slocum said. "Not that you're too stupid, but that it's too easy. What if . . . someone . . . wanted you both out of San Francisco?"

"Amelia!"

"Might be," Slocum allowed.

"She has been hounding Papa to change his will, to cut us out entirely. So far, he has resisted. If she had him all to herself for a week or two, there's no telling what he might do!"

"That makes it all the more important to find Michael and get back to San Francisco," she said.

"All right. Cloverdale is just down the road a ways?"

"Might be more than five miles, but certainly not much more. Mr. Crocker has a summer home there. Otherwise, there's nothing exceptional about the town. Get in and ride with me."

"I don't think you or your pa would appreciate my horse riding along in such a fine car," he said, seeing past the woman into the poshly furnished interior.

"Why, we, oh, you're right," she said contritely. "Then I'll ride with you."

"My horse is tuckered out. Go on ahead. I'll get to Cloverdale before you know it."

"I'll be waiting," she said, batting her long eyelashes. "I'll be waiting and I'll be very grateful."

The train chugged off. Slocum cursed himself for a fool—a damned fool—for not wheeling the sorrel around and going in the opposite direction.

He got to Cloverdale about an hour after Julia's train and found the woman anxiously waiting for him on the station platform.

"John, I'm so glad you got here. I was worried."

"I made good time," he said. He had not pushed his

horse too hard, but he had not dawdled, either. The truth was he had not looked forward to fetching Michael Porges again. The one time had been hectic and dangerous enough.

"Michael came here because he had a friend living nearby."

"Had?"

"I've learned his friend died of dysentery a few weeks ago. I don't know where he would go."

"Who was his friend?" Slocum asked, dismounting. He tethered his horse in front of the railroad station. Julia's train had pulled off on a siding where the engineer and fireman could oil and service the locomotive and wheels.

"Milo Roberts," she said, coming down the steps to stand beside him. Slocum was all too aware of the woman's nearness. He felt her heat and caught the scent from her clean hair and faint perfume and began to respond. Slocum tried not to think with his balls instead of his brains, but Julia made it difficult.

"Milo Roberts," he repeated. "A farmer? Rancher? Miner?"

"Miner. He had a small claim up in the hills. I think he panned for gold in the streams. I met him once or twice. His family was wiped out during the Panic, and I lost track of him and the others."

"Michael apparently kept in touch," Slocum said, seeing in the younger Porges something more. Michael tried to keep his friends, no matter how bad the hard times were. This was not something he had learned from his father. Slocum believed Nathan Porges capable of switching his allegiances according to how he benefited personally.

"Help me find him, John," Julia said, pressing against him. He felt her breasts crush slightly and could not move without putting his arms around her trim body. It felt good holding her, even for a moment. Then he pushed her away. Mores were not much different in Cloverdale than they were in San Francisco. He did not want to tarnish Julia's reputation with any public show of affection.

"You staying aboard the sleeper car?" He jerked his finger in the direction of the fancy passenger car. She nodded. Then she bit her lower lip, as if thinking hard, then stood on tiptoe to give him a quick kiss.

"Hurry back," she whispered.

Slocum scouted the main street of Cloverdale and felt he had seen the entire town. The place was so small it had only one general store and two saloons. Seeing the store would close in a few minutes, Slocum climbed the steps and went in. A woman with gray shot through her black hair looked up from her bookkeeping.

"Evening, ma'am," Slocum said. "I'm looking for a friend and wondered if you might have sold him some supplies."

"Who might he be? Or is it a she?" The woman looked at him with no sign of emotion.

"It's a he," Slocum said. This caused the woman to brighten visibly. "Name's Michael Porges. He was on his way to visit Milo Roberts up in the mountains."

"A shame about Milo," she said. "Sickness took him within a week or two, I reckon. You married?"

"Uh, no," Slocum said, taken by surprise at the question. The woman brightened even more and closed her ledger.

"What can I get for you?" She came around the counter, trying to look coquettish.

"Not many eligible men in these parts?" he asked.

"Not as good a prospect as Milo," she said, sighing. "You thinking on staying? Milo had a good claim, or he said he did. Now and then he'd come in with a few flecks of gold. Nothing too big but enough to pay for his supplies. 'Cept the last time. He never got the chance."

"You tell me how to get to Milo's camp?" Slocum asked. "I'd need supplies to get out there."

"Look it over. You might take it over and stay a spell. Cloverdale's not too bad a place to put down roots, if you know what I mean." She favored him with a smile and pressed her hair into place. Then she gathered some items she thought Slocum would need getting to Milo Roberts's claim. To the pile Slocum added some ammunition for both his Colt and Winchester.

"Eight dollars and a few odd cents. Make it eight, even," she said.

"How much did Milo owe before he died?" Slocum asked. The question caught her by surprise.

"Oh, not too much. Well, he owed almost ten dollars," she said.

Slocum counted off a pair of ten-dollar greenbacks from his poke and handed them to her. "Take this and settle Milo's account."

"You don't have to, mister," she said, staring at him with real appreciation. He doubted she got much business in the store. From the way she circled over him like some love-sick vulture, he guessed there weren't many eligible bachelors in the area.

"I know, but I want to. My name's John Slocum. And thanks for your hospitality." He gathered his supplies and tucked them under his arm.

"You come back any time," the woman said. "My name's Meg. Meg Riley."

"Miz Riley," Slocum said, tipping his hat. "I just might do that."

Slocum knew Meg Riley watched him as he walked down the middle of the street on his way back to the railroad station, and somehow he did not mind. Too many people tried to kill him. She was about the first who came across as open and honest in what she wanted.

That thought burning in his head, Slocum crossed the

railroad tracks and started up the steps to the rear platform of Julia's car.

He heard her inside and didn't want to spook her, so he called out, "It's me. Slocum."

He pulled himself up and opened the door. Julia had not lit any of the gaslights inside, but he had heard her moving around. Or was it her?

Dropping his newly bought supplies, he grabbed for his six-shooter and got it out as a shadowy figure at the far end of the car showed itself.

Slocum fired—an instant too late. Another bullet ripped the length of the car and crashed into his belly. Slocum took a step back, hit the iron railing and tumbled over to land heavily on the tracks behind the car.

He tried to get up but all strength faded and pain welled up in his belly. Gasping, Slocum collapsed. Above him he heard light, rapid footsteps coming, and he could not force himself to move to get away. Slocum waited for a second shot to rob him of his life.

12

Slocum used every bit of his strength to force himself forward like a scuttling crab. He lurched under the rail-road car as another slug ripped past him. He dropped to his belly, hurting all over and wondering why he wasn't dead. The sound of boots on the iron steps leading from the car caught his attention. He rolled onto his side and almost blacked out from the pain.

He barely remembered lifting his six-shooter and firing. The bullet ricocheted off the iron step and spattered his face with a piece of hot lead. But the bullet did more than that. It blew the heel off his attacker's boot, stumbling the man and sending him sprawling in the cinders of the rail yard. Try as he might, Slocum could not raise his six-gun for a second shot.

Slumping to the ground, he fought the red curtain of pain that radiated from his belly. Slocum remembered being gut-shot before when Bloody Bill Anderson had walked up, smiled, slapped him on the back with one hand and fired point-blank into his stomach with a gun held in the other.

"John? What's going on?" came a distant voice he struggled to recognize.

"Julia," he gasped out. "Look out. Killer. Someone tried to kill me. Kill you."

"Whatever are you saying? Come out from under there." Julia Porges hesitated a moment and then let out a gasp. "You've been shot!"

Hands pulled him feet-first from under the passenger car. Slocum fought but was weaker than a newborn kitten. Then he gave up entirely and surrendered to the blackness quickly replacing the red veil of pain. When he awoke he lay flat on his back staring up at a brocade hanging on the ceiling of the railroad car.

He tried to sit up but the pain doubled him over.

"Stay still," Julia said. "You'll be fine. The bullet shattered your belt buckle, tore through your leather belt and then ripped your jeans. If it had been an inch higher, you would be dead."

"And inch lower, I'd be talking in a higher pitched voice," Slocum said. He rubbed his belly and felt the nasty bruise there. Bruised but otherwise uninjured. Lady luck had ridden at his side once more.

"Who did this?"

"Someone aboard your car," he said, growing stronger by the minute. "I thought you had all the lights turned out but when I saw it wasn't you, I went for my gun. The intruder was faster."

"I doubt that. It was dark inside, you said. Could you see who shot you?"

"No," Slocum said. He thought a moment, then asked, "How bad does your brother want to be found?"

"You think Michael shot you?" Julia put her hand to her mouth. "It's possible. He blamed you for getting shot back in San Francisco. But I don't think he was mad enough to shoot you. He, well, he's not that kind of person."

"He doesn't want to go home, and I'm the one who's

likely to find him. If I'm dead, what would you do? Go back to San Francisco?"

"I . . . I don't know. Maybe. Probably. Yes," she finally conceded. "This makes me feel so guilty, John. You got shot because of me."

"Not if it was someone other than your brother." He heaved himself up, aching all over. The pain had gone but a more general soreness filled his gut now, expanding up into his chest. It would take a while to work out the bruise. Stretching like a cat helped, but he found anger burning away the discomfort even faster. Someone had tried to kill him and would have to pay for it.

"I just don't know, John." Julia sat beside him on the bed and ran her hand along his cheek. "I don't want to lose you, but what if it was Michael who shot you?"

"That'll be between us to settle," Slocum said. "Michael and me. Until I find out, though, I'm going to assume someone else is responsible." He heaved himself off the bed. Momentary dizziness passed and he stood. Picking up his gun belt he saw that he would have to repair it before he could use it again.

"I'll have a harness maker in town repair it," she said. "It's the least I can do."

"This will work for me," he said, shoving the Colt Navy into the waistband of his pants. Slocum winced. The gun butt rested on his bruised belly. He shifted it slightly until it rode more comfortably. Gunfighters he had known carried their six-shooters like this, but he had always preferred a holster.

"Where are you going? Stay and rest."

"I need to check out Milo Roberts's shack up in the hills," he said. "Your brother might be there, and if he isn't, I might pick up his trail."

"Be careful, John," Julia said. She hugged him. He felt his shirt turning damp from the woman's tears. Disengaging her, he took a few unsteady steps to the rear of the car, settled his six-gun again, then jumped down the steps and went to his horse. The bruise still aggravated him but wasn't going to slow him down much.

The first mile he rode was hell, then the pain faded to an old memory. By the time he reached Milo Roberts's camp, Slocum felt almost whole again. He checked the stars and figured it was close to four in the morning. Going this long without rest after being shot up was stark foolishness, but Slocum wanted an end to the hunt for Michael Porges.

Dark shadows and dim starlight hid most of Roberts's shack. Slocum dismounted, then hunkered down and listened for a few minutes. The normal forest sounds assured him no one sneaked up behind him. The gentle rush of a creek a couple dozen yards away showed where Roberts's had worked a sluice to eke out the few pathetic grains of dust he used to pay Meg Riley for his supplies.

From the cabin came no sounds at all. The chimney showed no fire burned inside, but Slocum couldn't find any place to peer in. No windows, although a few cracks in the walls might have provided peepholes if there had been light inside.

Opening the door cautiously, he drew his six-shooter and swung around, ready to fight. The small dirt-floored shack was deserted. Slocum found the coal oil lamp and trimmed the wick to get a pale yellow light filling the cabin. He searched the pitiful belongings and found nothing to show Michael Porges had ever been here. For all that, Milo Roberts had barely been here. A small diary showed his preoccupation with how much gold he took from the creek but mentioned nothing about relatives or friends.

Slocum smiled when he came to the back of the small diary and saw what Roberts had written about Meg Riley. He had been sweet on the woman but had been too shy to let her know. Tucking the small book into his left shirt pocket, Slocum made a final search of the cabin. To no avail.

The sky lightened enough for Slocum to thoroughly search the ground around the cabin. Again he found nothing to show Michael Porges had been here.

By the time he returned to Cloverdale around noon, Slocum was determined to leave Julia and ride on. There was nothing more he could do for her.

As he rode to the railroad station, he frowned. The luxurious rail car still stood on the siding but the engine was gone. Slocum swung out of the saddle and tied his horse's reins to the iron rail before going up the steps and knocking. Julia came to the door immediately.

"John!" she cried, throwing her arms around him. "You're back!"

"What happened to the locomotive?" he asked. She pulled him into the car and sat on the edge of the bed, looking up at him.

"The engineer got a telegram from the dispatcher recalling him to San Francisco. I have to wait until the next scheduled train comes along. They'll hook up the car and take me the rest of the way."

"Where?" Slocum asked. "Where are you going?"

Julia swallowed hard, her brown eyes welling with tears. "That means you didn't find anything, doesn't it?"

"I didn't find hide nor hair of your brother. Milo Roberts lived in the cabin, and there was hardly anything of his to show he was anything more than a placer miner obsessed with getting rich."

"I don't know what I'm going to do, John. You tell me."

"No," he said coldly. "You decide for yourself. Get used to it. I'm going to ride on, as I had planned from the start."

"But—"

"But nothing. Live your own life. Let your brother find

his own way. I don't know what holds you all together, but it's not love."

"It might be hatred," she admitted. "But it's all we've got."

"Good-bye, Julia," Slocum said, starting to leave. The woman grabbed his hand and clung to it. She pulled it to her cheek. Her tears touched his skin and his heart. He tried to pull free but found himself sitting beside her on the bed. Then she had his shirt off and fumbled at his jeans.

"Let's see how your wound is doing," she said in a tiny voice. "Oh!"

Her hand brushed across his manhood, causing it to stir. A momentary pang radiated through his belly and then he forgot about it. Julia slid off the bed to her knees and put her face down to his crotch. Her ruby lips circled the thick head of his shaft and she began licking, tonguing, sucking. Slocum grew steely hard.

"Don't," he said, his hands resting on the back of her head. His words said no but his body contradicted him. The more she mouthed him, the more desire burned in his loins. The bruise forgotten, he drew her up to him and kissed her full on the lips. They sank to the soft bed as Slocum and Julia both worked to get her clothing off.

Sunlight slanted in through the car window and bathed her white body in butterscotch warmth. Slocum bent and licked at one nipple and then the other. They both responded immediately, blood pounding into them and turning both into throbbing nubs. Then he started sucking on them. Julia moaned and sobbed and began to thrash about under him. Slocum slipped from one cherry-capped snowy slope to the other, his tongue never leaving the woman's tender flesh.

She tasted salty, tangy, exciting. Slocum wanted more of her. And he got it.

Their mouths locked and tongues duelled. As they

orally wrestled, Slocum ran his hand down the woman's heaving belly and worked lower into the tangled thatch nestled between her thighs. His middle finger curled about and worked into the moist crevice he found there. He thought Julia was going to throw herself off the bed when she began flailing around even more forcefully.

"More, John, I want more there. More than your finger. I . . . I want this!" She grabbed at his fleshy column and insistently tugged it toward the place where his finger roved restlessly in and out.

He did not immediately obey her. The taste of her lips, the way her tender body quaked as he moved over her, the passionate need building within her—and inside him—all caused Slocum to take his time.

He caught an earlobe between his lips, sucked and then gently nibbled. His finger slid free of her well-oiled interior and stroked across her slightly domed belly up to her breasts. He cupped them firmly, squeezing until Julia squealed in desire. And then he moved his hand back down between her legs.

"Take me, John. I want to feel you in me. Please, John, I need you so!"

His hand parted her willing thighs. He rolled over and positioned himself. Before he thrust into her, he looked down into her half-closed brown eyes and saw the lust he felt mirrored there. Her legs rose on either side of his body as she opened herself fully to him.

He levered forward, his hips moving forcefully. The tip of his manhood banged against her moist nether lips, parted them, and sank deep into her womanly core.

Julia gasped, lifted her rump off the bed and tried to grind her hips down into Slocum's crotch to take even more of his pleasuring fleshy dagger.

He slipped his hands under her body and cupped her taut cheeks, lifted her off the bed and then began moving back and forth in a rhythm as old as a man loving a woman.

Sweat pouring off him, Slocum moved faster and faster until he felt the pressure building like a strained boiler deep in his loins. The heat of her intimate flesh, the way she moaned, her beauty, it all worked to set off Slocum. He gasped, lunged, and spilled his seed. Julia lurched up, clawing at his back as the hot rush set off a new bout of ecstasy within her tense body.

They both sank to the bed, gasping for breath. Hearts slowing, they lay alongside one another without saying a word. Slocum wondered what drew this woman to him. Did she make love to him only to keep him hunting for her brother or was there some other spark Julia felt? He did not know, and that worried him.

He liked the times spent with Julia, but as before, he realized they were from two different worlds, socially and financially. He felt rich having a few hundred dollars in his pocket. The bedspread under their naked bodies was more than he had earned in a year. And what did they share? She could tell him about the latest cotillion and he would tell her about raising horses.

All they really shared was Michael Porges.

"I'll stick with you a while to see if we can find your brother," Slocum said. "Are you sure he came up here? There was no trace at all of him at Milo Roberts's place."

"He was here. I know it, John," she said, snuggling closer and putting her cheek against his chest. He felt her slow, even breathing now.

"He might have breezed through Cloverdale and gone farther north when he discovered his friend was dead." Slocum thought out loud. "What's the next stop along the way?"

"There's not much going north, at least not on Papa's railroad," Julia said. "He just completed a spur that goes over to the coast and ends at Fort Bragg. If Michael didn't turn around and go back—"

"He wouldn't," Slocum said with some surety.

"Then he went on to Fort Bragg. I don't know what is there, other than it's not San Francisco."

"We'll see about finding your brother there," Slocum said and mentally added this would be the end of the line, not only for the Porges railroad spur but him, too.

"John, do you hear that?" Julia leaped naked from the bed and began hastily dressing. "It's the train! We can hook our car up and continue hunting for Michael!"

Slocum heard the distant whistle and knew the moment was gone. He had floated along in a warm, content bubble. It never lasted. He hefted his gun and then saw that Julia had kept her promise about finding a harness maker to repair his gun belt. He tried it on. The fit was both familiar and different. He dropped his Colt Navy into the holster and practiced drawing it a few times until it settled properly on his hip.

"There, John, there it is!" Julia waved but there was no reason for her to do that. The stationmaster had already raised the flags to alert the train to stop. The locomotive screeched to a halt and crew jumped down to begin hooking Julia's rail car onto the end of the three cars already attached to the engine. A freight car attached behind Julia's car where Slocum loaded in his sorrel. By now, the horse had gotten used to this jerking, halting, rapid method of travel and hardly protested being abandoned to ride alone.

Slocum stumbled when the locomotive began pulling again. They were under way once more, heading for the end of the line.

"I missed getting any food," Slocum told her. "Do you think anyone aboard the other cars might be selling something to eat?"

"There usually is," Julia said. "I'm sorry, John. It never

occurred to me that you hadn't eaten. We could have—"

"What? And miss that?" he said, indicating the rumpled bed. He smiled and shook his head.

"Let's see what there is available," Julia said. She and Slocum opened the front door and made their way across the small metal platforms between cars. He opened what had been the last door in the train and slipped in, Julia following. Slocum smiled. At the far end of the car was a hunched over fiercely red-haired woman in a shawl peddling fruit from a wicker basket.

He took a few steps toward her and then paused. Something about her was familiar—and unpleasant. Slocum made no move for his six-shooter but felt increasingly apprehensive as he neared the old woman. She looked up and saw him. Her brown eyes went wide, and she pulled up the shawl to hide her face.

"Wait!" Slocum called.

The woman bolted, ducking through the door at the front of the car.

"John, what's wrong?" asked Julia, hanging on his arm.

"That woman," he said, not certain what to say.

"She just went into the next car. She's not going anywhere. We can catch up with her."

"She—"

Before Slocum could explain, Julia gasped and knelt on a seat, her head poking out the open window.

"John, it's Michael. I saw him. I saw him in the forest!"

13

"Where?" demanded Slocum, pressing in close behind Julia. He looked intently at the wooded area flashing past but saw nothing.

"It was Michael! I know I saw him," Julia said. "He was in the woods with someone. It looked like an Indian."

"You might have seen a reflection in the glass," Slocum said. The late afternoon sun slanted through the far windows and cast strange reflections throughout the car. The other passengers stared at them as if they had gone mad.

Slocum wasn't sure Julia hadn't—and he wasn't sure he had not gone crazy, too, even listening to her. He stepped back and hunted for the red-haired woman in the shawl. She had vanished and something about her struck him as familiar, and not in a good way.

Before Slocum could take a step toward the next car and find the old woman, Julia reached up and yanked hard on the emergency cord. The car lurched as the engineer vented steam and reversed the wheels, filling the air with the stench of burning steel and the sound of tearing metal.

Slocum stumbled and fell. Every muscle in his body protested as he stood. He belly was not yet healed, and the wound he had taken in the side back in San Francisco gave him a twinge or two now, as if he had opened the wound. He steadied himself and glared at Julia.

"Why'd you do that?"

"You have to go after him!"

"We're only a few miles outside Cloverdale. No one in town had seen your brother," Slocum said, trying to sound rational in the face of her need to find Michael.

"You don't believe me, but I *saw* him, John. He was out there and he looked like . . . a prisoner."

Slocum didn't know too much about the Indians in Northern California but they were mostly peaceable except for the Modocs up north. He had seen more than one newspaper headline in San Francisco telling of the fight going on between them and the Army, and how the Army was getting its head handed to it. But here, along the railroad route? He had heard nothing about Indian depredations, much less kidnappings.

"The Indians aren't likely to take your brother. They'd be more interested in someone like you," he said. Slocum immediately regretted saying that. Julia blanched and looked faint. She sank to the seat and shook as if she had a high fever.

"What 'n bloody hell's goin' on back here? Who pulled the emergency signal?" The conductor bustled up, looking self-important. His belly strained to pop the brass buttons on his tight uniform and his florid complexion told Slocum he had been hitting the bottle. As the conductor got closer, Slocum smelled the heavy scent of bourbon.

"Miss Porges wanted me to get off here," Slocum said.

"You the daughter of—" The conductor swallowed hard and motioned for the angry passengers to be quiet. He turned to Julia and said in a low voice, "You shoulda asked me to stop the train, miss. It's downright dangerous signalin' like that."

"I'll get my horse out of the freight car," Slocum said to the portly conductor, "and you can be on your way in a few minutes. The terminus is Fort Bragg?"

"It is. We should be there not long before midnight. Or were goin' to arrive 'fore this," the conductor said.

"You'll make it just fine," Slocum assured him. The conductor glared at him, not knowing how he fit into this puzzle and not wanting to say anything to irritate a man who might work for the owner of the railroad. Slocum took Julia's hand and told her, "I'll find Michael, if he's out there. I'll meet you in Fort Bragg as soon as I know something."

She looked up, her soft brown eyes imploring. For a moment, he actually believed she had seen Michael Porges and this was not going to be a wild goose chase. Then he hurried to get his horse unloaded and saddled.

As he swung over the horse's back, the train built up steam and rattled and clanked on its way. Slocum thought he saw Julia lean out and wave to him, but he couldn't be sure because he was staring at the passenger car immediately behind the tender. The old woman, shawl pulled tightly around her shoulders, also watched as he vanished from sight when the train rumbled around a bend in the tracks. He thought she made an obscene gesture but could not be sure since the steam from the locomotive smokestack blew back and obscured her.

Slocum considered riding after the train and settling the matter about the old woman once and for all, but then he knew that was a fool's errand. He was probably mistaken. Where had he seen her before?

Shrugging it off, Slocum turned back down the tracks and rode slowly, hunting for any spoor left by Michael or his Indian captors. The tribes in the area went under the general name of Pomo, which meant little more than "the People." Most tribes called themselves this, no matter what part of the country they roamed. Slocum tried to remember any hint of trouble with the Pomo and had to admit defeat. The Modocs around Linkville, Oregon kicked up their heels and killed a few bluecoats, and if they ventured this far south, Porges had a great deal to worry about if he was their prisoner.

Not expecting to see anything, Slocum almost missed the faint trail leading into the forest. He reined in, stared and then frowned. He jumped down and examined the ground on all fours. A man wearing boots had been accompanied by two wearing moccasins. The trail was fresh and in about the spot where Julia claimed to have seen her brother.

"I'll be damned," Slocum said. "She saw something. But was it Michael?" He knew the odds were against it, but overtaking the party shouldn't take more than an hour. That would settle the question and give him plenty of time to start toward the coast and Fort Bragg to report to Julia.

"Can't be her brother," Slocum said as he carefully followed the trail of crushed grass and broken twigs. When he got into the forest disturbed patches of pine needles and other small signs kept him on the trail. The spoor was faint, but he doubted the Indians and their traveling companion tried to hide the trail. Rather, they simply walked through an area where it was difficult to track.

Slocum made his way slowly, not wanting to lose the imperceptible trail. The sun eventually betrayed him, and Slocum had to camp for the night. Stumbling on the Indians by accident might be worse than anything he could do, especially since he did not know if they had taken Michael prisoner or he went along willingly.

Slocum snorted in disgust. He did not even know if he followed Michael. Julia thought she had seen his brother but the white man—or the man wearing boots—might be someone who only looked like him. The visibility had been poor, her sighting only a split second long and Slocum could not argue with the notion she had seen what she wanted to see most.

He unrolled his bedroll and spread it under a tree with

low-hanging branches. Sometime during the night it began to rain, and Slocum had to get his poncho out to keep dry. By morning he knew the trail would be erased thanks to the gentle drizzle that had fallen most of the night, but he kept on. He had to find something to report to Julia.

Having no other choice, he continued in the direction he had taken the day before and trusted the Indians would not double back or veer off the game trail. Before noon he came on a deserted camp. Slocum walked around, searching for any clue he could. The rain had obliterated much of the spoor but some remained to keep him on the trail.

He knelt by a burned out fire and saw the remains of a rabbit in the pit. Someone had rather daintily eaten of the rabbit. An Indian would have stripped it clean of meat, then broken open the bones to find the marrow. It wasn't much to go on, but it told Slocum no Indian had dined on that rabbit.

Circling the camp he found fresh footprints showing where no fewer than a dozen Indians had left. Mingled with them were the boot prints he had seen the day before. The rain had stopped before the Indians broke camp, giving him a good trail to follow now. No attempt was made to hide the course, so Slocum set off at a faster clip, hoping to overtake the party before sundown.

As he rode along, keeping the trail in sight, he considered why he was doing this. He didn't owe Julia anything. What they had done together was from mutual attraction. He had made no promises, and she had extracted none from him. As much as he might want to see her again, if he rode on and left her alone in Fort Bragg Slocum wouldn't feel too guilty too long.

But he did feel some obligation to her to find if her brother had been forcibly taken by the Indians. The tracks gave no hint about that. Slocum wasn't inclined to let any white man remain captive of any Indian band, if he could help it.

As he rode along he caught scent of a cooking fire before he spotted the camp. Dismounting, Slocum advanced on foot, as silently as any Indian through the forest. He came to a small clearing where nine Indians had set up their camp for the night. They had reached this spot some time earlier because they had gone hunting and had already returned with a small doe. Two men used their knives to carve it up while another stoked the large fire to roast it. The blazing fire was what had caught Slocum's attention.

In a few minutes, the odor of roasting venison made his mouth water. He settled down and carefully pulled bushes around him to keep from being spotted by anyone in camp. They seemed to be a peaceful hunting party, but he didn't see any white man with them. After a half hour of spying, Slocum reluctantly admitted that one of the Indians might have store-bought shoes. Many of the braves wore cotton shirts and canvas trousers like placer miners. They obviously had many dealings with white men and probably traded freely.

Slocum started to leave when dusk was thick enough to mask his departure but stopped when a loud voice echoed through the forest.

"I don't want to do that!" The man's voice carried a hint of whiny edge to it, a tone Slocum remembered well. The last time he had heard Michael Porges speak more than a word or two in pain, he had been drunk and self-pitying.

He was sober now but the self-pity remained.

Slocum parted the bushes and peered out, the camp now illuminated by the fires alone. It took him several minutes to spot the dark shape that was both huskier and taller than the others.

"You can't make me do that," the man repeated clearly

enough for Slocum to identify him: Michael Porges.

The braves on either side poked and probed him. Porges recoiled and started to stand, but the Indians grabbed him and pulled him down. One handed him something Slocum couldn't make out in the gloom.

"Are you sure it's not that rotgut you make yourself?" Porges asked.

"Good," one brave said.

"I've got quite a thirst," Porges said, his resolve weakening. Slocum saw the shadowy figure take a small bottle and quickly drink it. "Gah! That's awful!" Porges flopped on his belly and retched.

"Cures what ails you," laughed one brave. The other chuckled and joined the others around the fire.

Slocum waited for the second brave to leave the puking Michael Porges alone, but he remained at his side. It was impossible to tell if Porges was a prisoner or if the Indians were truly concerned for his well-being.

Circling until he was within a few feet of Porges, Slocum fell to his belly and wiggled forward. The brave gnawed on a hunk of venison and called out jokes to the others, but he remained near Porges. The young man was in no condition to eat tonight. He sat with his arms crossed over his belly and made piteous noises, as if he might die at any instant.

Slocum waited another twenty minutes, but nothing changed. The braves remained close and Porges gurgled and occasionally vomited. The first Indian returned and handed the young man a drinking skin.

"Will this poison me, too?" Porges grumbled.

"Drink. Good for you."

Porges did. He belched but did not throw up again. Slocum inched closer, staying low to the ground and waiting for his chance. He could call to Porges, but if the man was a prisoner, that would alert the Indians. Better to spirit him out of camp and find what was going on.

Slocum waited another five minutes before the Indian who had camped alongside Porges got up and went to the fire to get more venison. Without thinking, Slocum surged up, crossed the few feet separating them and then clamped his hand firmly over Porges's mouth.

The man struggled weakly. In Slocum's grasp, he could never hope to win free with such feeble tussling. Slocum dragged him back a few yards and got him in the brush where he could talk to him.

"Your sister sent me," Slocum said.

"Julia?"

"She's waiting for you in Fort Bragg."

"She came after me?"

"For the life of me, I don't know why. Come on. Let's get out of here," Slocum said, seeing Porges was not going to put up a fight. He had been the least restrained, most ill-guarded prisoner Slocum had ever seen, and now trailed along as docile as a lamb.

"You're the fellow who got me shot," Porges said, digging in his heels. "I don't want to go with you."

"You want me to throw you back to the mercy of the Indians? I saw them try to poison you."

"That wasn't poison. It was medicine. I've got stomach cramps real bad."

Slocum peered at Michael Porges through the darkness and tried to make out the man's expression.

"Come on," he said. "We'll get to Fort Bragg and straighten everything out."

"There's nothing to get straight," Porges said petulantly. "I don't want to see her."

"I don't care," Slocum said, losing his temper. "I'll deliver you to her. If you don't want to stay, that's between the two of you."

"You're sleeping with her, aren't you? I can tell."

Slocum considered punching out Porges, but he did not want to drag the young man through the forest. The Indians would figure out their bird had flown and come after him quickly enough. That is, if Michael Porges was their prisoner.

Too many questions went without answers, and Porges was not likely to give those answers voluntarily.

He grabbed Porges by the arm and pulled him along behind, like an unruly child.

14

Slocum was glad to be at the end of this particular trail. He had done too much already finding Michael Porges, and for nothing. There was no sense of accomplishing anything, even if he had a dozen questions burning on his lips.

Porges struggled feebly but came along until they were a hundred yards away from the Indian camp.

"How'd you tie up with them? And what tribe are they from?" Slocum asked, turning to face Porges. The blow hit him squarely on the forehead, knocking him back a step and stunning him. The second blow landed across his eyes and blinded him. Slocum grabbed for his eyes where the rough-barked limb had smashed his face. Then the world went away as the heavy wood club crashed down on the top of his head.

The water dripping onto his face brought Slocum around. He sputtered, rolled to his side, and felt nothing but pain filling his head. Head and body, he decided. There was not a square inch of his body that didn't hurt like hell. The rain fell in a soft drizzle, not enough to soak him but enough to be annoying. Slowly piecing together what had happened, Slocum regained his senses and opened his eyes a little to see if he was in even hotter water than he thought.

His field of vision was limited, but he saw no Indians. Shifting his weight slightly, he got his hand on his Colt Navy, rolled onto his back, drew and cocked his six-shooter. Slocum found himself pointing his six-gun at empty air.

"Son of a bitch!" Slocum growled. He got to his feet. His head felt as if it had been split open. If he hadn't been wearing his Stetson, the wound might have been worse. Slocum found a broken branch a few feet away and, from the fresh blood on it, knew this had been the weapon used to knock him out.

His vision cleared and he turned in a full circle, hinting for Porges—or the Indians who had recaptured him. Slocum was alone in the forest.

He shoved his six-shooter back into its holster and then allowed the dark rage to fill him. Nobody cold-cocked him like this. No one, be they white or red got away with it. He had told Julia he would return her brother, but if Michael had been the one to ambush him, Slocum was not sure the young man would be returned alive.

And if the Indians had jumped him, Slocum vowed eternal vengeance on them.

Fury sharpening his skills, he circled where he had been slugged and found a trail leading back in the direction of the camp where he had rescued Porges. Slocum threw caution to the wind and ran back to the now-deserted camp. The fires were cold and much of the debris had been piled to one side of the clearing. The Indians were long gone and with them, Michael Porges.

Slocum knew he could go to Fort Bragg and tell Julia he had lost track of her brother. Or simply ride on and wash his hands of the Porges family. Or he could go after Michael Porges.

He had begun this out of a misguided sense of honor for Julia Porges. Now Slocum sought the woman's brother for his own reasons. Eyes like an eagle, he found the Indian trail quickly and saw they angled inland and over the mountains toward Yreka. The local Pomo Indians were peaceable, but Slocum got the feeling these were on the run. The trouble with the Modocs to the north worried him a mite, since Michael Porges seemed drawn to the worst of all possible circumstances. Where worse to go than the middle of a full-scale war?

Slocum got his horse and started on the trail, his anger feeding on itself every time he touched his battered face or a new pain jammed itself through his head.

The Indians had traveled fast for four days. No matter how Slocum worked, he could not overtake them. From the way they laid out their campsites, from the bits of gear they lost or left behind, he suspected they were Modoc. As he rode, he tried to figure out why Michael Porges rode with them because the young man had been responsible for the attack. The more Slocum thought about it, the more certain he was that Michael Porges had swung the branch and knocked him out.

The Modocs might be light on their feet, but they would have left a trail back to their camp. Slocum had seen only Porges's tracks. And after that, the group rode together. He might have missed a single brave—or Porges—departing the band, but he did not think he did.

"Why did you join them?" grumbled Slocum. It made no sense to him. He rode through rain and good weather and the distant mountains grew closer day by day. Mt. Shasta rose majestically and Slocum rode past, heading to the northern California border. And still he could not quite catch up with the fast-moving Modocs.

The fifth day on the trail marked a difference. Slocum lost the trail. The Modocs began hiding their tracks, as if they finally realized they had a man coming after them.

As he knelt and studied the trail where the Modocs had gone into a small stream, Slocum heard the clank of metal on metal and the sounds of many horses. He started to find a place to hide and wait to see what was going on, then stopped when he heard a bugle and saw a white and blue battalion pennon fluttering through the trees.

Cavalry.

Slocum waited rather than going to ground. A few minutes later the gold-braided officer spotted him and signaled his sergeant to halt the column. The officer commanded more than twenty soldiers, all who looked like battle-hardened—and battle weary—veterans.

"What are you doing in this area?" the captain called in way of greeting.

"Good day to you, too, Captain," Slocum said. The officer inclined his head in the direction of the stream. The soldiers broke ranks, half watering their horses while the other half watched and waited to be sure their comrades weren't caught in a trap.

"You ride up from the south?"

"Came from San Francisco," said Slocum, figuring this was as good an explanation as the captain needed.

"You're in extreme danger here."

"Do tell? I've seen evidence of some Indians—"

"Modocs," the captain interrupted. "They're on the warpath."

"But nothing to worry about," Slocum finished.

"Captain Jack is a tough hombre," the sergeant spoke up. "You ought to heed what Captain Hodges is saying."

"How far from here is the fighting?" Slocum asked.

"Not that many miles," the captain said. "Many Caves at the south end of the Lava Beds is only a day's ride."

"Don't know the country," Slocum admitted. "Maybe you could tell me what's going on."

"Captain Jack's the Modoc chief, and he's upped and

killed General Canby. Murdered him under a truce flag. We're trying to flush the red bastards out of their stronghold in the Lava Beds."

"You reckon any of them got away from your patrol and went south?" asked Slocum.

From the dark expression on the captain's face, Slocum knew the answer. This patrol was supposed to stop trafficking between those inside the Lava Beds and those out. Michael Porges might have thrown in with Modocs returning with much needed supplies to help their brothers' war against the white man.

"Have you seen any Indians, sir?" the officer asked coldly.

"Nope," Slocum said honestly. "Not in a week or more, and then I saw some down south, near Cloverdale."

"Pomos," the officer said, as if the name was bitter on his tongue. "A worthless lot."

"Not killers like the Modocs?"

"No."

The captain wheeled his horse and rode away without another word. The sergeant moseyed over and waited until his commander was out of earshot.

"You got to excuse Captain Hodges. He lost his brother during the Battle of Lost River. Modoc sniper killed him first thing. His brother never had a chance, and it's made the captain mighty bitter."

"I can understand that," Slocum said. "Why would any white man throw in with the Modocs?"

The sergeant squinted at Slocum. His leathery face wrinkled up as he considered his answer and why Slocum might have asked it.

"Them folks over at Yreka like the Modocs, especially Captain Jack. They treat him like royalty, mostly because Jack lets his women go to town. Whores. The bunch of them are whores." More than a little bitterness came into the sergeant's words. Slocum wondered if he had lost friends or relatives in the battle, too. Probably.

"Should avoid them," Slocum said.

"A good idea. Avoid them all, and if you hear chanting, ride like Lucifer's demons are after you. The Modocs are following Wovoka's Ghost Dance rituals."

Slocum had heard of it and how it scared so many military men. Wovoka promised a return to the old days, when the Indians roamed freely and hunted vast herds of buffalo. If the white man died, or so said the tenets of the dance, all Indians killed would be resurrected and live forever.

"It's more than just a protection against bullets, isn't it?" Slocum asked.

"That's part of it. Cures what ails you, if you're an Indian," the sergeant said. The bugler shouted to him, then put the bugle to his lips and blew assembly. The sergeant left Slocum where he stood, more curious than ever—and more determined to find Michael Porges.

Slocum let the column ride on, then headed straight north, for the southern end of the Lava Beds. If Porges still rode with the Modocs, that would be their entry into the volcanic stronghold.

The land turned rockier, then became almost impassable. Sharp black volcanic rock littered the area and afforded few paths through it. Slocum got to a rise and looked north. He shuddered at the sight of unbroken rock that looked like the waves on the ocean. To go down into the ravines and gullies meant losing sight of the horizon. He would be cut off from anything but the sun above—and the rain clouds forming would quickly blot out the sky.

"Where are you?" wondered Slocum, scanning the land for any sign of the Modocs and Michael Porges. He smiled in triumph when he saw a tiny curl of smoke rising from a fire not a mile off. The sun was going down, and the Indians might have thought their cooking fire would not be spotted.

Slocum homed in on it like a bloodhound, only to find there was no direct path. The rock-strewn trail twisted and turned and dipped low into ravines, as he had feared. He finally dismounted and advanced on foot, not trusting himself to ride in the twilight through such unforgiving terrain. He didn't want his horse getting cuts and bruises on the legs. To be stranded on foot meant added danger.

"You'd better have a damned good explanation," Slocum said under his breath, wondering what possible excuse Porges had for running off the way he had. Slocum trudged along and suddenly came to a clearing in the rock towering on either side of the trail. He backpedaled fast to keep the Modocs from spotting him. A dozen Indians sat around a single fire, near a stack of what Slocum took to be supplies intended for the Modoc's chief, Captain Jack.

Leaving his horse some distance back down the trail, Slocum advanced on foot. He had no intention of taking on the braves, especially since they might be alert for cavalry patrols, but he wanted to see if he could figure out Porges's situation.

Slocum quickly found sneaking up on the camp was difficult because of the treacherous tumble of sharp-edged rocks. He managed to get within twenty feet of the Modocs and had to content himself with spying on them from here. Now and then one brave walked slowly past on sentry duty, but he could not see Slocum where he crowded into a dark niche in the rock. If a man knew the lay of the land, it might be impossible to pry him out.

Slocum did not envy the Army their attempts to fight the Modocs in this perilous country.

After the guard walked past, Slocum edged out of his hiding place again and crept closer, narrowing it down to one of two men who might be Michael Porges. When one spoke fluent Modoc, Slocum knew the other had to be Porges. For the life of him, he could not see the ne'er-do-well son of a railroad magnate learning an Indian tongue.

The sun had set and the moon would not rise for another half hour, plunging the land into inky darkness. Slocum walked on eggshells across the clearing to where the man he had identified as Porges slept, wrapped in his blanket.

Remembering what Porges had done to him down south, Slocum considered the best way of getting him away from the Modoc camp.

As chancy as it was, slugging Porges and then dragging him out seemed the best plan. Slocum drew his pistol and judged distances. For a plugged nickel, he would put a bullet into Porges for all the trouble he had caused. But he drew his Colt back to wallop the young man alongside the head. Before he hit Porges, he heard the soft sound of moccasins moving against the ragged rock.

Slocum couldn't run without being seen. The guard couldn't miss with an easy shot to Slocum's back. And to fight it out meant he would awaken the entire camp and find himself shooting it out with more than a dozen Modoc warriors.

The guard called out a challenge. Slocum froze, wondering what the quickest way of dying might be.

15

Slocum couldn't fight and couldn't run, so he decided to hide—in plain sight. He dived forward and flopped down next to Michael Porges. Porges stirred, grumbling at the disturbance. He pulled up his blanket enough to shield Slocum from direct view and never knew it.

"What's goin' on?" the young man called. The Modoc guard said something in his own language. "I don't understand," Porges said petulantly. "Speak English."

Slocum clutched his pistol and waited to be found out when Porges sat up and looked at the guard. Remaining still, Slocum wondered if he looked like a lump in Porges's blanket.

"You okay?" asked the guard.

"There's nothin' wrong," Porges said. "Just trying to get some sleep, but you woke me up." He whined a little, but Slocum no longer cared. This satisfied the guard, who wandered off to patrol the clearing in the middle of the volcanic rock hell.

Porges tugged at his blanket and found Slocum was on top of it. For a second, Porges relented, then swung around and faced Slocum.

"Who're you?" Then Porges recognized Slocum.

The time for action had come. Slocum swung awkwardly and hit Porges alongside the head with his pistol barrel. Stunning Porges was easy but keeping the small fight private was not. Porges cried out and tumbled back onto his blanket. Slocum swung again but missed, hitting a rock near Porges's head.

The Modocs began stirring, disturbed by Porges's outcry. Slocum knew he could remain and find himself in hot water or he could take the slim chance he had right now to get away. He had only a split second to decide. Hating it but seeing no other way, he scuttled like a crab and found a pile of the sharp-edged rock to hide behind. An instant after he hit the ground and curled up to conceal himself, the Modocs found Porges and how he had been stunned.

Slocum huddled behind the rock and waited for the Indians to come after him. But they didn't. Porges was groggy and stuttered out his story of being hit by someone who had just appeared at his side. The Modoc sentry shouted and waved his arms like a scrawny bird flapping to get itself airborne. Then the argument started—but no one came after Slocum. He decided they believed Porges had fallen and hit his head on one of the rocks.

Either that or they figured it was a fool's errand trying to track anyone in this wasteland. The rock left no footprint and hunting at night was a one-way ticket to a grave. Ten minutes later, Slocum relaxed and knew the Modocs were not coming after him. But his dilemma remained. How could he pluck Porges from their grip?

Why did they give him sanctuary when they were locked in a bloody war with the Army?

Slocum settled down and waited, alert that the Modocs did not spot him. A little before dawn, he heard them striking camp. He poked his head up and watched their dark silhouettes packing and leading their horses to the north, toward the heart of the Lava Beds. The band vanished quickly, and Slocum cursed. He threw caution to the wind and dashed back to where he had left his horse nervously waiting.

He swung into the saddle and turned the sorrel's face back toward the clearing. Slocum wasn't sure how he was going to track the Modocs through this rugged country, but he had to try if he wanted to find Michael Porges and get him to safety.

As Slocum rode through the clearing where the Modocs had camped overnight, he reined in and stared. Porges's blanket was where it had been, and a lump showed the young man was still underneath. Slocum worried the Modocs might have slit Porges's throat and left him. He trotted over and looked down.

Porges stirred and sat up, rubbing his eyes.

"What's going on?" he asked sleepily.

"Your friends left you, and you're headed back to your family," Slocum said.

Porges surprised him by ducking beneath the sorrel's belly, then slapping the horse on the rump to make her rear. Slocum fought to keep from being bucked off.

"It's not going to work, Porges. We're going to Fort Bragg. Your sister's waiting for you there."

Slocum got his horse under control and slowly turned in a full circle. Porges had vanished as if he had never existed. Slocum walked slowly in the direction Porges must have taken. He caught his breath when he saw where the young man had taken refuge. A small crevice twisted about and led to the other side of a ridge.

Dismounting, Slocum forced his way through the razor-edged cleft in the rock. Instead of finding himself on the other side of the rocky ridge, Slocum stumbled and slid down an incline into a chilly cave. All around he saw evidence that Porges had come this way. Drops of fresh blood on the edged rock showed Porges had cut himself, and in the distance came faint echoes of feet pounding on the ground.

"Porges!" Slocum shouted. "You're going to hurt yourself bad. What's wrong with seeing your sister again?"

Slocum started slogging through the muddy patches on the cave floor, wondering where the water came from. A few feet from the crevice cut off even the faint light of dawn. He banged his head on a dirty chunk of dangling ice and recoiled, painfully finding the source of the water. Slocum rubbed his head because pain had shot through his entire body, reminding him how Porges had clobbered him before. Anger burned brighter now and kept Slocum on the man's path.

Tracking Porges was easy until he came to a narrow branching. The light was completely gone, and Slocum progressed by feel. Knowing he could guess wrong and be lost forever in the cave if he found enough dividing paths, Slocum took the time to fumble out his tin of lucifers and strike one. He immediately saw where Porges had gone. Bloody hand prints marked the right branch.

"Porges, don't make me come after you. You'll die in this cave. The Modocs left you behind and you don't know the country. I can get you to safety."

"You won't take me to my father?"

"Julia is waiting in Fort Bragg," Slocum called. Porges's voice echoed slightly but not from too far off. He swore when the lucifer match burned his fingers. Slocum lit another and saw Michael Porges a few yards deeper in the cave. The young man shivered as if he was freezing to death—or struggling with some vast problem.

"I suppose it's better with her than with my father," he said. This comment struck Slocum as odd, but he said nothing that might talk Porges out of cooperating.

"I'm running out of lucifers." Slocum waited a few seconds and struck another. He had five left, and he hoped to use them to light a cigarette or two. Backing away toward the cave opening had the desired effect of drawing Porges with him, like a moth to a flame.

By the time Slocum had gone through three more lucifers, the pair of them were outside the ice cave in the cold dawn light.

"I shouldn't go with you. I need to be cleansed, and the Modocs promised me."

"What?" Slocum stared at Porges. "What are you talking about?"

"I am filled with demons that are eating my soul. The Ghost Dance can drive them out. I had thought to go to Mt. Shasta and use its mystical power to cleanse my soul, but the Modocs found me."

"What mystical power?" Slocum asked, in spite of himself. "It's only a mountain."

"No, no," Porges said with a pathetic eagerness, as if he had to share this with someone. "There is a cosmic power that flows through it. Mysterious things happen around it. I had hoped this power might drive away the darkness wrapping around my soul."

"Don't drink until you're in a stupor," Slocum said harshly. "Don't drink at all. You can't hold your liquor."

"I drink to forget," Porges said, shoulders slumping. "I am so weak."

"We finally agree on something. You have a horse or did the Modocs take it?"

"Over there," Porges said, pointing. The two men walked to a natural corral where Porges's horse nickered and occasionally kicked at the rocky walls. "They took all the supplies. I had hoped the Ghost Dance would cure me."

Slocum knew there were sicknesses other than of the body. He had seen men so mean they would kill for the thrill of seeing another die. He had seen men laugh as they tortured others—and worse. But Porges seemed weak and venal rather than cruel.

"You bought ammo? Or food?"

"Ammunition. They said this was needed most. For hunting," Porges said.

"Yeah, for hunting," Slocum scoffed. "They're fighting the Army and from what I heard, they murdered an Army general under a truce flag. You supplied ammo to the wrong side in a nasty little war. They are hunting, all right, but for soldiers and maybe the settlers all around the countryside."

"They are so spiritual, they can help me get free of her." Porges shuddered, then wiped away the beginnings of tears welling in his eyes. "Now they've left me, what am I going to do, what, what?"

Slocum wondered what Porges was talking about. Then he figured getting free of "her" meant steering clear of his stepmother. Amelia Porges was likely to put poison in her stepchildren's food to get rid of them. In a way, Slocum thought Michael running off served both their interests. If Michael stayed away from San Francisco, he no longer had to fear his stepmother's wrath and her control over his father, and Amelia Porges got free rein to spend her husband's vast wealth.

"You're coming with me to Fort Bragg," Slocum said.

"I need to cleanse my soul," Porges said piteously.

"When we get to Fort Bragg, you can find a preacher," Slocum said. "Give away your money, if that makes you feel better. There are any number of things you can do with your life to make yourself feel good."

"You don't understand," Porges said.

"No, I don't," Slocum said, not wanting to. He was fed up with the young man's weakness and whining. For all the strength and brains he found in Julia, it was all missing in her brother.

They rode slowly to the south, heading away from the Lava Beds. Slocum was glad to see them vanish on the horizon as they angled away from the region. Slocum saw

Michael looking over his shoulder in the direction of Mt. Shasta and worried the young man might take off for the mountain and its strange restorative powers. But Michael rode along, slumped over and looking like a whipped dog.

Slocum wondered if he had enough money that he would turn out like this. He doubted it because he had common sense. In general, money did not ruin a man. It only intensified the traits already in a man's heart. He had seen too many children of rich men to believe they all ended up like Michael Porges. Something had gone wrong in this man's childhood to break his spirit. Growing up with a man like Nathan Porges for a father would not be easy, but it ought to have given Michael a spine of steel, not one of flexible, floppy tule reeds like those growing in so many of the marshy areas around them.

"How long have you felt this . . . lack?" Slocum asked, not knowing what the exact description ought to be. He felt he had to figure something out about Michael to anticipate any escape he might make.

"Eight," Michael answered without hesitation. "I was eight. And it got worse after that. I need to purify myself. Do you know how to do a Ghost Dance and drive away the evil spirits?"

"No," Slocum said, clamping his mouth shut. He had wanted to make conversation and wile away the long hours in the saddle. He changed his mind. All Michael Porges could do was repeat the same tired things over and over.

"Railroad tracks," Michael Porges said fearfully. "These belong to my father."

"Probably," Slocum said. They had spent the last week making their way south and west, heading for Fort Bragg on the coast. Crossing the mountains had been a chore until they found a pass and then had come down to find

the tracks. From here it would be easy to follow them into
the town where Julia waited.

"I . . . I don't want to go. My sister is there."

"If you try running, I'll put a bullet through your leg.
If you try to escape again, I'll put a bullet in your other
leg and strap you belly-down over your saddle. You and
Julia are going to be together before the sun sets."

Slocum wondered at the way Michael turned pale at the
idea of this small family reunion. As they got closer to
Fort Bragg, he saw the reason. On a railroad siding sat a
fancy rail car and a powerful locomotive that seemed out
of place for a logging town.

He glanced at Michael, who stared at the car.

"My father's personal Pullman car," he said in a choked
voice. "You're bringing me to him!"

Porges jerked at the reins and got his horse wheeled
around and into a full gallop back in the direction they
had just traveled. Slocum heaved a sigh, turned his sorrel
and went after him. Porges was scared and not thinking.
His lathered, straining horse faltered within a mile. Within
two Slocum was catching up and by three had closed the
distance between them. Taking his lariat, Slocum worked
out a loop and began swinging it over his head.

Michael was trying to push his horse beyond the limit
of its endurance and paid no attention to anything hap-
pening behind him. Slocum swung his lariat and then
loosed it. The loop fell around Michael's hunched shoulders and tightened as Slocum slowed. Porges flew from
the saddle and hit the ground hard.

Slocum didn't feel too sorry for him. He remembered
the way Porges had hit him with the branch and had led
him such a chase through the ice cave. As if he worked
a balky calf, Slocum backed his sorrel and kept the rope
tight around the feebly struggling man.

"Give up, Porges. It's not worth it."

"No, you don't understand what he'll do to me!"

"I'm not turning you over to him this time," Slocum said. What should have been reassuring words turned Porges into a tiger. He fought hard, but Slocum had him securely roped. Slocum jumped to the ground and worked his way along the rope kept taut by the hardworking sorrel. Using his knife, Slocum cut off a few feet of rope from the free end and in a few minutes had Porges hogtied and bound.

"I'll leave you here and see what's going on in town," Slocum promised. "A little scouting won't hurt."

If he expected any gratitude from his captive, he was disappointed. All Michael Porges did was whimper.

16

Slocum approached the fancy railroad car on foot, cautiously peering through a window into the posh interior. He had thought the car Julia had ridden in from San Francisco was luxurious. This one might have been ripped from some Eastern pasha's palace. Gilt everywhere glittered from gaslights and doorknobs, cut crystal in the windows, and fancy paintings on the walls bespoke of immense wealth.

But the car's owner was nowhere to be seen. Slocum climbed the steps at the rear of the car and opened the door. Heat boiled out from inside and the blazing lights blinded him. He swung into the car and closed the door behind him. At the far end a Franklin stove churned out enough heat to broil a trout. Porges obviously liked it hot when he traveled.

Slocum sat at the railroad magnate's writing desk and pawed through the papers strewn over it. He wasn't sure what he was hunting for but thought he would know it if he saw it. All Slocum found were invoices and bills dealing with the railroad operations. Lots of them. Many were stamped with red ink stating they were overdue. How Nathan Porges ran his business affairs didn't matter to Slocum. The man might be rich because he never paid on time.

If Slocum had been a thief, he could have made off with a small fortune in paintings and furniture, but nowhere did he see any greenbacks or gold coins lying around. The rumpled bed near the stove showed Porges had been aboard recently and the maid or whoever straightened up after him had not made it. This bothered Slocum. A man like Porges never traveled without a herd of servants.

What had happened here?

Slocum saw no hint of foul play. Nathan Porges had simply walked out and gone into town. If he wanted to find the engineer or fireman and ply them with a few drinks, Slocum might get a more complete story about the trip here. Or not. Porges had not been forthcoming when he hired Slocum to fetch back his son the first time. There was no reason to think he shared the reasons for his travel with a lowly railroad engineer.

A last quick check of the car revealed nothing to pique Slocum's curiosity, other than why Porges had come to Fort Bragg. It was the end of the line for his railroad— did Nathan Porges also consider it the end of the line for his daughter since she had run off to find Michael?

Answering that question required more than poking about in the rich man's belongings. Slocum left the car and rode another half mile into Fort Bragg, following the tracks. Although he came across several more sidings before he got to the main rail yard, he didn't see Julia's car. He had hoped to locate her and get the matter of her brother settled fast so he could be on his way.

On the ride to Fort Bragg from the Lava Beds, he had thought hard on Michael—and about his sister. Julia was a lovely woman but not the kind who could hold Slocum for long. They had dallied and it had been good, but Slocum was getting itchy feet and was ready to move on.

At least, that's what he told himself. Deep down, he was fed up with the Porges family and the hidden currents sweeping them all up in a torrential flood.

He left the rail yard and headed into Fort Bragg, which was slowly coming alive for the night. Loggers and men making their fortunes sending wood down to San Francisco for the booming construction there crowded into the rows of saloons lining the two major crossing streets. The street running parallel to the nearby ocean seemed the most active, so Slocum headed along the boardwalk in search of anyone able to tell him where he might find Julia Porges.

Slocum poked his head into one saloon and looked around the smoky interior. He almost headed in for a beer or even a shot of whiskey when he saw how cheerful the customers appeared. Being on the trail for almost a week with Michael Porges had soured Slocum on human companionship, and this saloon offered the chance to renew his faith—a little—and to wet his whistle.

He pushed through the swing doors and looked around for a spot to sit down. Slocum blinked, not trusting his eyes. He thought he was wrong and moved closer to the woman at the bar, clinging to a logger and whispering in his ear. From the way the man grinned, Slocum figured it had to be a lewd suggestion.

The woman wore the same clothing as the old woman selling food aboard the train. But she moved in a sprightly fashion and was anything but old. She turned and thrust out her chest. As she did, she grabbed the logger's hand and placed the meaty paw directly on one of her ample breasts.

"Like it? You can have the whole shebang for a dollar."

"Florrie?" Slocum called, remembering the crazy whore who worked the docks back in San Francisco. She had put him onto Michael Porges's trail. But what was she doing in Fort Bragg?

The woman jerked about. Her eyes went wide when she saw Slocum. Her grip on the logger's wrist tightened, and she pulled him around so he stood between her and Slocum. Then she shoved him hard so he stumbled back and crashed into Slocum.

The men crashed to the floor, Slocum's breath knocked out by the heavy man landing squarely on top of him. Gasping, gagging a little, Slocum got to his feet and fought to get air back into his lungs.

"Mister, I'm sorry," the logger said. "Didn't mean to knock you over like that. The danged Cyprian shoved me, and I lost my balance. Lemme buy you a drink."

"That's all right." Slocum got out. Florrie was long gone. She had been out the back door before he had hit the floor. She might have wanted him in San Francisco but now she obviously sought to avoid his company.

"No, no, I insist. I'd take it as an insult if you didn't accept."

"Put that way, how can I refuse?" Slocum wanted to avoid a fight with the man, who was already several drinks ahead of him in the race to get drunk. "You see her before?"

"The whore?" The logger shook his head. "She was a wild one, but I never seen her before, and I been in Fort Bragg for well nigh a year. Cut redwoods. You got the look of a hard worker about you. Needin' a job? We always want good workers."

"Let's talk about it over that drink you promised," Slocum said, sidetracking the man. He knew how backbreaking the labor of lumberjacking was and had no reason to seek a job now. But he was thirsty and the man was buying. Slocum spent the next hour listening to the logger tell about cutting down redwoods and cutting them into planks for sale down south as far as Monterey.

The man's attention began to fade, and Slocum finally walked away without raising the man's ire. Slocum stepped into the cold night and tasted the salt in the air coming off the Pacific. The fresh air cleared his head. He wondered at seeing red-haired Florrie in this saloon, but stranger things had happened to him—and recently.

Slocum continued his hunt for where Julia might have gone. He had to admit she could have taken her car and returned to San Francisco, but something in his gut told him she wouldn't. She had said she'd wait for him to fetch her brother. The way she had spoken made Slocum believe her determination to help Michael outweighed anything Nathan Porges might say to her.

Even if he threatened to cut her off from his fortune.

Slocum went into the middle of the street and looked around, trying to get his bearings and figure out where Julia might be holed up. Much of the vast amount of the lumber cut in the hills above the town was sent south on ships, but the railroads had to carry a significant portion of the boards. He might have missed a siding or even an entire rail yard where her car might have been pulled aside.

He stared at one brightly lit dance hall doorway and knew Florrie had poked her head out to see if he was still on her trail. Slocum had no real interest in the woman, save that the incident with her in San Francisco had been strange. She had sent him to the very spot where Michael Porges had been shanghaied and might have been part of Captain Greer's scheme to impress sailors.

"Hey, you!" she shouted. "Want some more? Come and get it, if you got the balls for it!" She threw back her shoulders and lifted her blouse, showing him her bare breasts. Then Florrie laughed insanely and ducked into the dance hall. Slocum took an involuntary step forward, then stopped. He had no business with Florrie. If he had seen her on the railroad selling food, and he was positive now it was the crazy woman pretending to be an old woman, that explained when she had come to Fort Bragg.

Why she had come didn't matter to him. People drifted from one town to another in the West. Just like Slocum.

Slocum passed the dance hall and walked the length of the street until he left the bright lights and boisterous sounds from the saloons behind. Small boardinghouses where someone like Julia might stay lined the road now and stretched off on side streets in either direction, some heading down precariously to the ocean and the rest stretching uphill toward the forests. He could ask after Julia but doubted any reputable proprietor would tell a scruffy looking drifter like him about a single woman staying in a decent house. The hotels he had seen were not the kind of place a woman of Julia's wealth and tastes was likely to stay.

"Where would she put an entire railroad car?" he wondered aloud. There was no reason she would find a place to sleep in town when she had such a fine car. He turned and went back toward the rail yard. The tracks running into the hills told him he had found a local route, not one of Porges's main lines. Slocum retreated to where Porges's car was parked and saw he had missed a pair of tracks heading to the north away from Fort Bragg.

Slocum followed the tracks until they branched. One line headed into the deep forest, possibly a competing line to the California Western Railroad for the business of hauling logs from higher in the mountains. The other set of tracks looked more promising when Slocum found a few empty freight cars and a coal tender waiting for repair work along it. The sidings were filled with rolling stock all carrying the Porges company name.

A few shacks on the single set of tracks showed him where Porges's repair men stowed their equipment. Slocum poked through two of the shacks and saw nothing interesting. Disheartened with his lack of success, Slocum stepped outside again. He put one foot on a rail and felt distant vibration. Peering north he saw faint light filtering through tree limbs and headed in that direction.

Julia's car came into view, parked at the end of the line. Only a single kerosene lamp burned inside, unlike her father's brightly lit, overheated car. Before Slocum reached the back platform, he heard low voices coming from inside the car. He immediately recognized Nathan Porges's rough voice, but the other was muffled and indistinct. Rather than barging in, Slocum went around the car trying to eavesdrop and see what he was getting himself mixed up in.

He wasn't tall enough to see into the windows, so he hunted for a box to stand on. Slocum felt like a peeping Tom as he dragged an empty dynamite crate over and stood on it. Inside the car he made out Nathan Porges's bulky form. The railroad magnate waved his arms and then yelled out, "You're insane! This is no good. I thought you had stopped. She was right about you. I can't believe it. I can't!"

"Oh, Papa," came Julia's soft voice. "You're so old fashioned. You don't know what you're talking about. Amelia has poisoned you against Michael and me."

"Poisoned! She's an angel compared to you!"

Slocum saw Julia stand and move about, cloaked in shadows. Nathan Porges spun around and the two of them huddled together. Slocum shifted his weight on the crate to get a better view since he could not figure out what they were arguing about. If he saw what the father and daughter did, it might give him some clue what the argument was about and how Michael fit in.

The battered crate began to creak under his weight, forcing Slocum to jump down. He went to the rear of the car and stared at the closed door, wondering what to do. He came to a quick decision. He would bull in without knocking. It was impolite but it might startle the two into revealing what this was all about. From the snippets he had overheard, he felt the blowoff was near, and he wanted to know where he stood so he wouldn't get blown up.

He started for the side of the car to climb the metal steps when he heard a humming coming from the direction of Fort Bragg. He had felt vibration on the rails earlier and had found Julia's car, but it was stationary. The freight cars on the sidings along the tracks had been empty and as still as the grave. Whatever caused the rails to hum was not produced by any of the rail cars Slocum had seen.

He turned to see a handcar racing along the track, a dimly seen figure working hard on the pump handles. The handles rose and fell as the car sailed down the track toward the rear of Julia's car.

"Hey, stop!" Slocum called, taking a step forward. He waved his arms to attract attention. Slocum didn't know if the handcar had a brake, but there must be some way of slowing it down. The car sped on until it was only a few feet away from him. Slocum dived off the tracks an instant before the empty handcar crashed into the rear of Julia's car and shattered into a thousand splinters.

If he had stayed on the tracks, he would have been caught between the passenger car and the handcar. Slocum didn't see any way he could have escaped being killed when he realized how completely the handcar had been demolished by the collision.

Picking himself up, Slocum turned angrily to see who had sent the handcar into the passenger car, almost killing him.

A dark shape rose from beside the tracks and blossomed like some evil flower as a cloak spread out. Slocum's gut turned cold. He didn't see the gun but sensed it being aimed at him. A shot tore past his head, sending his Stetson sailing. The second shot was even more accurate.

17

Slocum grunted as the second bullet slammed into him, hit Milo Roberts's diary in his shirt pocket, and then hotly touched his bare flesh. The bullet should have killed but the thick book saved his life. A cold fury burned in him as his hand flashed to his six-shooter and drew. He fanned off three quick shots and was rewarded with a shrill yelp of surprise as he winged his attacker. The dark figure turned and hightailed it for the far side of the rail yard, giving Slocum the chance to cock his six-gun again, aim, and fire. The fleeing man tumbled to the ground, rolled lithely and came to his feet still able to run. The range now was too great for a handgun, but Slocum emptied the cylinder at his attacker.

When the hammer fell on a spent chamber, he grunted again and pressed his hand to his wounded side. He could never run fast enough to catch the man who had tried to crush him, then shoot him. Slocum winced and examined his side. The bullet had found almost exactly the precise spot where he had been injured back in San Francisco. This time the wound was trivial but it hurt like hell and oozed sluggishly from the single round spot where the bullet had sneaked through the diary and cut into his flesh.

"What's going on out here?" bellowed Nathan Porges, bustling from the back door in Julia's air car.

Slocum said nothing, more intent on his wound. Seeing that Porges was not going to leave him alone, Slocum gave up trying to tend the tiny pockmarked wound and turned his attention to reloading. Staying around the Porges family had proven mighty dangerous.

"I asked you a question!" Nathan Porges came over, chest thrust out belligerently and with an expression on his face that forced Slocum to use all the restraint he had. A good left to the chin would not only deck Porges, it would give Slocum great satisfaction.

"Someone tried to kill me," Slocum said, finishing the chore of reloading. He shoved his six-shooter back into his holster and faced Porges squarely.

Porges blustered and harumphed but Slocum's cold gaze backed him down. A little.

"Why are you here? Spying on me?"

"Yes," Slocum said, too fed up to sugarcoat his answer.

"Why, how dare you!"

"That backshooting son of a bitch tried to kill me, but I think he was following you," Slocum said. "Might be his luck is better next time."

"You are meddling in my family's personal affairs, and I do not like it."

"Papa, please," Julia said, coming up beside her father. She was flushed and looked radiant. Somehow, this time her charms had no effect on Slocum. "I am sure John was only trying to help. Weren't you, John?"

He started to tell her he had Michael hogtied and waiting in the forest but held back. The way Nathan Porges acted kept him from showing his hand too early. Besides, he had fetched Julia's brother because she had asked, not because Nathan Porges cared.

"John? You call him 'John?'" Porges turned on Julia. "When did you get so familiar with a man I hired? Are you this forward with all the men in my employ? Amelia was right about you two! I knew it!"

"I am not a whore, Papa! Not like Amelia!"

Slocum's hand moved like a striking snake as he grabbed Porges's wrist. The railroad magnate's strength surprised him—or was it his own weakness? Slocum staggered a little but kept Porges from striking his daughter.

"I'll have you arrested, Slocum. I swear I will," Porges said angrily. "No, not that. I'll have you strung up! By God, I don't know how, but I'll see your heels kicking in the air."

"No, you won't," Slocum said, his words as icy as Porges's were hot. "If you try hitting Julia again, you won't be seeing anything because you'll be dead."

Porges jerked free of Slocum's grip and stalked off. Every time his boots hit the cinders in the rail yard, the crunch turned into a sick grinding sound, as if Porges imagined Slocum's face under his soles. Slocum said nothing as Porges headed in the same direction taken by his assailant. Let them shoot it out. Let the bushwhacker kill Nathan Porges. For all Slocum cared, let the entire Porges family get shot.

"John, I'm so sorry," Julia said, lying her hand on his arm. He pulled away. "What's wrong?" she asked.

"The more I try to do for you, the more I get shot up. And I don't even know what's going on."

"Oh, you are wounded. Let me clean the gunshot and put a bandage on it."

Slocum let her lead him to the car and tend his new injury. Once Slocum would have enjoyed having the lovely brunette's fingers stroking over his body, even with a wound giving a fair amount of discomfort, but not now. He was too fed up with everything that had happened since the night when Nathan Porges had hired him to track down his wayward son.

"You're mighty quiet, John," Julia said, putting a piece

of gauze over the small round wound and then fastening it into place with adhesive tape. "There. All patched up."

"Thanks."

She looked at him closely. Her lips thinned to a line as she turned away from him.

"I'm sorry Papa acted so badly. He came up here on business and found that I was here waiting for you—for you to bring back Michael."

"I don't care how rich he is, if he keeps acting the way he did he's going to get a bullet in the belly."

"You, John? You'd shoot him?"

"The temptation is there," Slocum admitted, "but I wouldn't kill a man in cold-blood. Your pa rubs me the wrong way, and I'll lay you odds that I'm not the only one."

"You're right. He came up here to find why the railroad lost a valuable contract shipping logs south. Without it, the railroad is in serious financial trouble."

"Bankruptcy?"

Julia nodded, looking concerned. "You can see why Papa is so upset. It's not with you. It's not even with me or Michael. His entire fortune is at stake."

Slocum smiled humorlessly and said, "That means he's likely to lose Amelia."

"I don't know about that," Julia said glumly. "She's a leech, a barnacle on his hull that even loss of money can't scrape off. Her lot in life is to make him—and me—miserable. She—"

"So Porges is fighting for his financial life," Slocum cut in, not wanting to hear the rest of Julia's diatribe against her stepmother. As frightening as the prospect of losing the family fortune was to Julia, Slocum was not sure it mattered that much to Porges. He had worked his way up from poverty before and could do it again. Something more sparked the man's disagreeable confrontation with Slocum.

What it might be, other than Amelia's bogus claims, Slocum had no idea, but he thought the railroad magnate used his wife's lies as an excuse rather than believing them. Porges's family was about the least loving and loyal Slocum had ever seen, but then the railroad tycoon had done nothing to deserve more from them.

"Amelia," Slocum said, a thought drifting around at the fringes of his mind.

"Forget her, John. She doesn't deserve your worry."

"I—" Slocum clamped his mouth shut. It wasn't in his nature to worry about a gold digger, but there was something more that refused to come into focus for him. He pushed it aside. The sooner he turned Michael over to Julia's care, the sooner he could reach Oregon and get to raising Appaloosas. Somehow, though, this seemed more like a pipe dream than a possibility to him.

"Forget all that," Julia said. "Papa will figure out something. He always does. I need to know if you found Michael." She read his expression and clapped her hands together gleefully. Then she bent over and impulsively kissed him. "Good, good!" she cried. "If anyone could find him, I knew it was you. This is so good. I ought to reward you."

She closed her eyes and her lips parted seductively. Slocum felt himself responding to her overtures but this time he kept himself in control.

"There's no time for that," he told Julia. "Michael didn't want to come on his own, and if the cavalry ever caught him, he'd be in a world of trouble."

"What's he done now?"

Slocum told her quickly of her brother's involvement with the renegade Modocs and how he had bought ammunition for their war against the U.S. Army. He finished with a description of how he had left Michael Porges tied up.

"Oh, the poor thing," she said almost gleefully. "He must be so frightened."

Slocum frowned. Julia spoke of him as if he were a small child. She saw his displeasure and laid her hand on his arm.

"It's just that Michael can't care for himself. He needs someone to look after him. If Papa were more of a father, he would tend to him, but he ignores Michael entirely, so it's up to me." Julia heaved a deep sigh. "It has been that way ever since Mama died."

Slocum pulled his shirt on and stretched a little. The pain in his side was not too bad and wouldn't slow him down. From earlier experience with the other wound, he knew he could ignore the injury entirely once he got to riding. Once he was away from the Porges family, he might be able to ignore the pain entirely.

"You have a horse?" Slocum asked.

"I can get one in Fort Bragg. Is Michael far?"

"Not too far. I came on into town when I saw your father's rail car. It doesn't pay to walk into a fight unless you know what you're up against." As Julia hurried to get a few things thrown into a bag, Slocum pondered his own words. He found himself chin deep in something he did not understand at all.

Together, they left the railroad car and went into town. Slocum got his horse while Julia sweet-talked one from the livery stable owner. While she was gone, Slocum mounted, feeling every muscle in his body protest. He had been beaten and battered and shot more than once during the past couple weeks. Riding was something of a chore, but by the time Julia trotted up on her borrowed mare, he felt better. Not ready to tangle with his weight in wildcats, perhaps, but better.

As they rode down the street, heading out of town, Slocum got the uneasy feeling of being watched. His side throbbed, as if reminding him of his brushes with death.

Looking around, he tried to spot anyone obviously interested in him or Julia, but the town was bustling with activity and no one appeared to be staring at them. Still, the feeling that he was being watched refused to go away.

"It'll be so good seeing Michael again," Julia said brightly. She smiled winningly and seemed to come alive at the idea she and her brother would be reunited.

"He's not too eager to see anyone in his family," Slocum said, choosing his words carefully. Then he decided the best course was bluntness, as it had been with Nathan Porges. "He doesn't want to see you."

"What? Don't be silly, John. Of *course* he does. He's my brother."

"I'm not sure he won't bolt and run when I set him free. If he does, you're on your own tracking him down again."

"I understand. You've been so understanding. I do want to thank you properly." Julia batted her eyelashes and smiled wickedly at him, even lewdly. Slocum's heart would have raced faster at such a look once. Not now. All he wanted was to be somewhere else. Anywhere else.

"Why does Michael want to avoid you?" Slocum asked.

"Oh, he doesn't. He is such a mixed-up person. Ever since our mama died, he has been at loose ends."

"He acts as if he's afraid of you," Slocum said, pressing the point. Julia's reaction told him she was going to lie to him.

"He's not afraid of me. It's just that I want to bring him back into the family. It's Papa he feels who has been cruel to him."

Slocum slowed their ride, then stopped entirely so he could look back along their trail. He had left Michael Porges tied up three or four miles outside Fort Bragg and they were getting close to the spot now. But the feeling of being watched never went away, not for an instant since they had ridden from town.

"What's wrong, John? You're as jumpy as a long-tailed cat next to a rocking chair."

"Might be I'm getting jumpy in my old age," he said. "Or overly cautious. You wouldn't know if anybody was following us, would you?"

"I—no, John. The only one who might is Papa, and he blunders about like a bull in a china shop. Subtlety isn't his strong suit."

Slocum agreed with that. If Nathan Porges had been the one who had smacked him with the tree limb instead of his son, it would have been expected. The railroad magnate was about that subtle. But he controlled a far-flung railroad and had hundreds of men working for him, any of whom might be capable of tracking without being seen.

Slocum was a good tracker and knew all the tricks for covering his trail, but he had found more than one Indian who was better. There might even be a white man with more skill.

"Let's get on with it, John. Where's Michael?" The sharp edge to Julia's voice told him he was right. He pointed to where her brother was, then he rode on.

"Up this draw, then at the top of the embankment. I tied him to a tree, a tall one. In the dark it was hard to tell what kind, but it had distinctive branches. From a distance it looked like an old man reaching out."

"How gruesome," Julia said. "How deliciously gruesome for Michael."

Again Slocum wondered about the Porges family but held his tongue. He rode up the draw and spotted the tree silhouetted eerily against the night sky. A puff of wind made the branches sway as if a blind man was groping to find his way.

"That's it, isn't it, John?" she asked. Slocum saw the way her breasts rose and fell under her starched white blouse as excitement seized her. Julia snapped the reins on her mare and got the horse moving faster, as if she couldn't wait to be reunited with her brother.

"I see him," Slocum said, dismounting and tethering his sorrel at the bottom of the draw. He didn't want to risk the horse stumbling on the slope in the dark. Slocum slipped on pine needles and dried leaves but made his way to the tree where he had hogtied Michael. The young man stared at him with wide, fear-filled eyes.

"You had to bring her, didn't you?"

"She's your sister," Slocum said.

"Yes, Michael, I'm your sister. Now be quiet while Mr. Slocum cuts you free."

Slocum reached for his knife but heard something behind him, half turned and then stumbled and fell, rolling down the steep slope to the bottom of the ravine when a well-aimed bullet caught him high on the shoulder. This time Milo Roberts's diary wasn't in the right position to save him from a serious wound. He was still conscious as he tumbled ass over teakettle but he hit his head on a rock and never saw the back-shooter who had gunned him down.

Head ringing and pain surging throughout his body, Slocum passed out.

18

"Wake up, wake up," Slocum heard from a distance. The roaring in his ears died down a little, but the pain refused to go away. "Please, wake up. We're in trouble, John."

"Where am I?" Slocum tried to sit up, but the pain forced him to collapse to the ground. He blinked and saw nothing. Slocum panicked, thinking he was blind. Then he realized he was under a low-hanging limb. A shrub with leaves blotted out his vision.

"The forest, where you tied up Michael."

"Julia," Slocum said, things falling into place now. He felt where the bullet had struck him. Every time he sucked in a breath, his body filled with liquid fire. Moving was out of the question.

"Yes, yes, John. We can't stay here. Whoever shot you is still out there."

"Where's Michael?"

"I don't know. Up the hill, where you left him. I don't dare go see. I might be shot!"

"How bad am I hit?" Slocum tried to examine himself but his arms had turned to lead. Breathing was a chore but got easier as he worked on it. From the location of the pain, he had been hit in the left shoulder. Slocum reached over gingerly and touched the front of his shirt, and his fingers came away wet. The bullet had entered him from the rear and gone clean through his shoulder.

Rather than weakening him, it fired him up. He had been shot and beat up and this was the last time he would take it. The wound was clean and the bullet had passed entirely through him, leaving his left arm well nigh useless. That meant he had to do all his shooting with his right hand, which suited Slocum just fine.

"Patch me up," he ordered Julia. "You took care of the other wound. This isn't that much worse."

"There's no bleeding. I don't think anything important was hit."

"There's bleeding inside," Slocum said. "I can feel it. You're going to have to cauterize the wound."

"Burn you? But the dry-gulcher is still out there. And Michael! He needs me to—"

"Go on, then," Slocum said angrily. "I'll take care of the bullet wound myself." He wasn't too surprised to see Julia stand, as if she was going to leave him. Then she dropped back to her knees beside him, a look of consternation on her face. He was forcing her to do something against her will and it did not suit her.

"What do I do?"

"Get a fire started. When a twig about the size of the bullet hole gets to burning, shove the stick into the wound until the flesh chars."

"Oh, John, that's so . . . ugly."

"Do it." He sagged back, mustering his strength for the pain he knew was ahead. But it had to be done, backshooter roaming the forest or not. He felt the liquid slipping of muscles and blood vessels in his shoulder. In spite of what Julia said—or hoped—he needed immediate attention or he would die.

Even if he got it, he might die. Why hadn't their ambusher come after them? The shooter had the upper hand with Slocum wounded. Slocum knew he dared not dwell too long on the would-be killer's motives until he got the drop on the man. Then he could decide whether to pull the trigger and end the murderous son of a bitch's life or turn him over to the law.

At the moment, Slocum was tending toward meting out justice personally.

"I found your lucifer matches," Julia said with no enthusiasm. "A few leaves and dry twigs ought to do for the fire, right?"

"Do it," Slocum said, closing his eyes and focusing on his anger. It kept him alert and his mind off the pain in his shoulder. The sharp, acrid scent of burning leaves came to tickle his nose. Then Julia moved closer and knelt beside him.

"Here it goes, John. Get ready."

"Do it."

Slocum ground his teeth together as Julia stuck the flaming hot wood into his shoulder wound. He felt the heat closing off bleeding veins inside. He shuddered and then was aware of her pulling the fiery shaft out.

"There, it's done."

"No, it's not," he said. "You have to do the back, too." He rolled onto his side. Julia grumbled and said very unladylike things, but she repeated the crude treatment. The pain almost caused Slocum to black out, but he hung on to consciousness, grimly determined to go after his assailant.

He took short, quick breaths and felt better in a few minutes. Still weak as a newborn kitten, Slocum sat up. He shook as he reached over, took his left hand and tucked it inside his shirt front to keep it from flopping about. Slocum looked up and saw Julia staring at him, wide-eyed.

"You've done this before, haven't you?" she asked.

"This isn't the first time I've gotten shot," he said. "It

won't be the first time I let the gunman get away with it, either."

Slocum got out from under the bush and leaned against a tree until dizziness passed. He was in no condition to go hunting for a backshooter but it would rankle more if he didn't. Drawing his six-shooter, he turned and started back up the slope to where he had left Michael Porges tied to a tree.

"John, be careful," Julia urged.

He said nothing. She could come with him or hide. It didn't matter. Slocum dug his toes into the soft forest dirt as he made his way up the steep slope. The gunman had shot him from somewhere on the other side of the ravine, but Slocum wasn't interested in picking up that trail when he knew the bait—Michael Porges—was likely to have been taken.

Three-quarters of the way up the slope, Slocum's legs gave out under him. He dropped to his knees to keep from tumbling backward. Determination was sufficient to keep him going only so long. He had to rest. Then Slocum felt an arm around his waist, helping him up.

"Thanks," he said to Julia.

"I have to see after Michael," she said anxiously. This put everything into perspective for him. Slocum knew he was expendable to her after he served her purpose of getting her brother back. He dug in his boots, rocked forward, and got moving again.

He reached the top of the ravine and started off a game trail a few yards to where he had left Michael Porges tied up. Slocum wasn't surprised to find only cut ropes left behind.

"He's gone!" Julia moaned. "Find him, find him, John. Track him down!"

"Whoever shot me has him," Slocum said, stating the obvious. If he had not gotten free in the hours Slocum had been gone, chances were against him wiggling out of the ropes in the past few minutes. More than this, the ropes were cleanly cut, showing Porges had not escaped on his own.

"That way. I see the way the pine needles have been shuffled around on the ground." Julia lacked real skill as a tracker but the trail was as obvious as the sunrise. "Come on. What are you waiting for?"

Slocum experienced a flash of weakness, then nodded. He had to see this through. Wary of a trap, he started on the trail like a bloodhound. Gripping his six-gun, Slocum was ready for anything but what he found a half mile off.

He topped the ridge and found a small clearing. Michael's hands were still tied securely. And brazenly forcing herself on him sexually was Florrie, the red-haired San Francisco whore he had seen in Fort Bragg and on the train.

19

"Help," cried Michael, struggling to get away from Florrie. "Help me. Please!"

Slocum wondered what he had gotten himself into. There was no reason on earth he could figure that the San Francisco harlot had shot at him only to drag off Michael Porges for her sexual servicing. She had never been shy and must have attracted every sailor in San Francisco, not to mention every logger in Fort Bragg.

But there was something about the way she moved, looked, acted that kept gnawing at the edge of Slocum's mind.

"Look out!"

Slocum was not certain if the warning came from Michael or his sister, but it wasn't needed. He saw the metallic gleam of the small pistol in Florrie's hand and already surged forward to deal with the threat. His good hand closed around her wrist and forced the muzzle away. Then Slocum realized he had misjudged the woman's strength and determination. She fought like a cornered rat. With only one good hand and a body filled with pain from the shoulder wound, it was more than Slocum could do to fight her.

Twisting around, Slocum forced her to drop the gun. She came at him with her fingers curled into vicious claws and went for his face and eyes. Slocum stepped back, let her stumble past and then considered what he could do. Standing and letting the whore disfigure or kill him was not one of the possibilities Slocum considered. He whipped out his six-shooter and swung it, connecting with the side of the woman's head.

The blow knocked Florrie to the ground but did not stun her. Like a wildcat, she swarmed up and came at him again.

"I should have killed you in San Francisco. I should have killed you in Fort Bragg. I hate you!"

Slocum had his six-gun pointed at her but the woman rushed for him, oblivious to the danger. He saw how completely insane she was from the way her eyes were wide and specks of foam came from her mouth. He had seen mad dogs that looked more reasonable.

"I'll shoot," Slocum warned and then it was too late. Florrie crashed into him and bowled him over. He dropped the six-shooter and grabbed at the woman to throw her aside. To his surprise he caught a handful of red hair and it pulled free. Slocum stared at it and wondered how he had scalped the woman.

Slocum looked up and then everything fit together. She wore a cheap red wig. And he had seen Florrie before. Demented and snarling, Amelia Porges came for him one more time. Slocum dropped the wig he had pulled off the woman's head, judged distance, and swung with his good hand. He winced as his knuckles connected with the point of Amelia's chin, knocking back her head. She crumpled to the ground, unconscious before she hit.

Panting, Slocum stood over her and stared at the carefully applied dirt. It was as if Amelia had put on fancy makeup instead of the dirt, but she had applied it like an actress puts on stage grease paint to change her appearance. With the wig changing her hair color, it had been an effective disguise.

"What is going on?" Slocum gasped out. He spoke to thin air. Julia had rushed to Michael and was hurriedly freeing him of the ropes still binding his wrists.

The drama between brother and sister was as confusing to Slocum as finding out that the wife of one of the richest men in San Francisco dressed up and sold herself as a whore along the docks. Michael edged away from Julia, but the young woman threw her arms around him and held him close. Then she kissed him, and it wasn't a sisterly kiss.

"What's going on?" Slocum shouted, at the end of his patience. "This is your stepmother. Why'd she get all dressed up like that?"

"She's not responsible for what she does," Julia said, still hugging Michael close. The young man looked like a trapped animal ready to run for the protection of the brush.

"She tried to kill me!" Slocum froze when he heard a six-shooter cock. His eyes darted to where his Colt Navy lay on the ground. Then he saw Florrie's—Amelia's—pistol a dozen feet beyond.

"I don't want to shoot you in the back, Slocum, but I will. I swear I will."

"I wondered where you were, Porges." Slocum did not turn around. He wanted to make it hard for Nathan Porges to gun him down, but Slocum figured the railroad magnate would overcome his squeamishness about shooting a man in the back in a few seconds.

"I wish you hadn't found out about Amelia," Porges said. Slocum heard the man's boots crushing leaves behind him. Porges was within ten or fifteen feet of him. Too far to turn and fight, even if Slocum was up to it. All the fighting with Amelia had taken its toll on him. His shoulder sent sharp jabs of pain throughout his chest and made his left arm totally useless.

"Why does she dress up like a cheap hooker? Isn't she getting what she needs from you?" Slocum knew he played a dangerous game baiting Porges, but he had no choice. Trying to talk reasonably with Porges was a long-dead choice. He had to force the man into making a mistake. The only problem with Slocum's impromptu plan was that all the outcomes seemed to end with him getting a bullet in the back.

"She was an actress before we married," Porges said almost plaintively. "Not a very good one, but she thought she was as good as Kate Denin or even Felicita Vestvali." Porges snorted and Slocum could imagine the man shaking his head. "She *was* like one reviewer said of Madame Vestvali. 'Ponderous proportions and minimal talent.' But she's my wife and I love her."

"So you'd kill for her?"

"Yes, Slocum, I would. No one must know she is . . . like this."

"Deranged? Crazy as a bedbug?" Slocum pushed hard now to force the man into a mistake.

"She can't help herself when she gets like that. She . . . she turns into a different woman, one of loose morals. My position in San Francisco society is too tenuous. Those snobs who live on Rincon Hill have never mingled with anyone living on Nob Hill. They think we're all Johnny-come-latelies with our wealth we worked for. We didn't inherit it. We worked for it. *I* worked for it!"

Slocum heard the shrillness coming into Porges's voice and knew he had only seconds to decide how to get away alive.

"Papa, please," Julia said, still clinging to her brother. "He doesn't know anything. Who'd he tell?"

"He has to know. He found out her secret."

"Everyone wishes they were someone else sometimes,

Porges," Slocum said. "I'm not going to tell anyone."

"Not even the police?"

"Papa, shut up!" cried Julia. "He doesn't know Amelia kills the men she seduces when she's like this."

Slocum felt sweat break out on his forehead. He had been lucky after he had been with Florrie—Amelia. Then he realized how their liaison had been different. He had asked after Amelia's stepson, the very same Michael Porges she had been having her way with while he was tied up.

If he had stepped into a den of rattlers, Slocum could not have felt colder inside. Or sicker to his stomach.

"I never gave in to her, Father," Michael Porges spoke up. "She tried to seduce me but I never let her. Not like—"

"Shut up," snapped Porges. "I don't want to hear what's gone on between you and your sister."

It all fell into place for Slocum. Amelia was not the only one with problems in the Porges family. The ebb and flow of animosity revolved around power and sex as much as it did money.

"I don't want to do this, Slocum, but I have no choice. What you know is going to be buried with you on this spot." Slocum heard Porges stepping closer. From the corner of his eye he saw salvation coming from a peculiar quarter.

Amelia Porges had regained consciousness and inched toward him. As Porges spoke, the lunatic woman's attention had been shifted to her husband. With a loud inarticulate cry, Amelia got to her feet and launched herself through the air toward Nathan Porges.

Slocum ducked down as a bullet ripped past his head. He hit the ground hard and rolled, going for his sixshooter. Pain turned his fingers clumsy, but he fumbled and got the ebony-handled Colt Navy up and aimed. But he hesitated.

Amelia and Porges struggled. She used her fingers like claws on Porges's face as she had tried to do to Slocum. Porges pushed her back, but Amelia screamed madly and rushed him again. This time he raised his gun to fend her off. The two went down to the ground in a heap. The muffled report of Porges's gun sounded. And then the railroad magnate and his wife went limp on the ground.

Slocum walked to them, his six-gun aimed and ready to fire. He didn't care which of them had been shot since both had wanted him dead. But he saw Porges lying on his back and sobbing. Slocum knew what the outcome of this brief, fierce, mad fight had been. He stepped closer and kicked the gun from Porges's hand.

"I killed her," Porges sobbed. "I loved her, and I killed her."

Slocum knelt by Amelia's limp body. At long last she seemed at peace. That might have been because she was very, very dead.

"Papa," Julia cried, hurrying over to kneel by her father. Slocum saw how Michael Porges edged away, eyes darting to the edges of the forest and the possible refuge he might find there. Slocum felt nothing but contempt for the young man. He tried to escape his family but not very hard. If anything, Michael Porges had "escaped" in such a fashion that he would be found and returned.

It turned Slocum's stomach.

Almost as much as staring down at Julia and her father.

"Let him be," Slocum said. "He doesn't need your help."

"He's my father," Julia said angrily.

Slocum saw from the slackness in Porges's face that the man's spirit was broken. He might recover. There was a hard core to him that had fought and scraped and scratched to get to the top of the railroad business in California. If Nathan Porges succeeded in finding that determination again, he could get through this. Slocum really did not care.

"You and Michael get on back to Fort Bragg," Slocum said, a wave of tiredness washing over him. He had reached the end of the trail and didn't want to go any farther. But he had to, at least for one more distasteful chore. "Take your father with you." Slocum turned and pointed his six-shooter at Michael, who had crept a few yards toward the dubious safety of the trees.

"What will we tell everyone?"

"You'll figure out something. Porges can't run his railroad in this condition. You'll have to do it for him, you and Michael. And you'll have to come up with some story explaining what happened to your stepmother."

"We can do that," Julia said, her eyes glowing. Slocum knew he had dangled a carrot in front of her. She would control a railroad, even if it was near bankruptcy, and it would give Julia power few women ever saw. What she would do with—or to—her brother was between them.

"We can say Amelia ran off with a theater troupe," Michael said. "Her friends know she was on the stage."

"It will make her seem like she's the villain and Papa the victim," Julia said, relishing the tall tales they were beginning to spin. "A pixie out to do the wonderful man harm. We can make them believe it, except—" Julia looked up at Slocum. The calculating look told him he had to walk carefully around her now. She had tasted power and wanted to exercise it. If he crossed her, Julia would make sure he ended up as dead as any of Amelia's dockside lovers.

"I'll bury Amelia here," Slocum said. At the words, Nathan Porges began whimpering and curled up in a tight ball on the ground. He muttered something over and over, but Slocum paid him no attention. Let him dwell in his self-caused pain. It was punishment enough for what he had done in his life.

"Do you want Michael to help? He would like that. He never liked Amelia." The steely edge to Julia's words made Slocum's blood boil, but he held in his anger. It was up to Michael to stand up to his sister.

Slocum saw the young man was not going to do it. Michael's shoulders slumped and Slocum expected him to ask if he ought to fetch a shovel to help dig the grave.

"Never mind. It'll take both of you to get your father back to his rail car," Slocum said. "You might want to stay there a while until you work out a story you can remember."

Julia's eyes flashed at this insult, but she said nothing to him. She motioned to her brother to help her get Nathan Porges to his feet. The man shook as they walked away, crying uncontrollably. Nathan Porges tried to break free and return to his dead wife but his children kept him walking out of the clearing. Slocum watched them vanish.

He felt as if a weight had been lifted from his shoulders.

He turned back to Amelia Porges and dragged her to a spot at the edge of the clearing where the ground was softer and easier to dig. Using a broken, dried tree branch to scratch in the ground, Slocum finally dug a decently deep grave. He rolled the woman's body into it and then looked down at her.

Amelia Porges seemed at peace. At long last, she of all her family was at peace. Slocum crossed her cold hands on her breasts, dropped a delicate blue-petaled wildflower into the grave, then began pushing the dirt over her still form. When he had a mound built up, Slocum piled large rocks atop it to keep the coyotes and wolves from digging up the body. He doubted anyone would come along, see it, and wonder who had been buried here. Too many men died and were buried where they fell for anyone to get curious.

Slocum wobbled from the exertion and sat down on a lightning-struck tree stump. He reached up and touched his blood-stained shirt, fingers tracking the outlines he found there. He had a pocket filled with greenbacks, more bullet wounds than he wanted to count, and a book that had saved his life back at Fort Bragg when Amelia had tried to crush him with the handcar and then shoot him down. And memories. He had burning, vivid memories of the woman he had just buried and her stepchildren and her husband.

Slocum spat. Then he got to his feet and headed back to find his sorrel. He knew where he had to go.

The train clacked by, but Slocum ignored it. He rode down the main street, head swiveling from side to side as he hunted for the woman he wanted to find. She wasn't out on the street, but he had not expected that. Slocum knew where to find her.

He dismounted in front of the Cloverdale general store and went inside. From behind the counter Meg Reilly looked up. Her broad, sincere smile brightened the store.

"Well, stranger, I wasn't expectin' to ever see you again," she said. "What can I do for you?"

"Don't think too badly of me," Slocum said, sitting down. He was still weak from his shoulder wound. "I found this diary out at Milo Roberts's place and didn't give it to you right away. It's got some things in there about you."

"You read it?"

"That's how I came to think you'd like to have it. Sorry about the blood stains."

"Your blood?" Meg eyed him carefully.

"The book saved my life over in Fort Bragg," Slocum said.

"Then it served a good purpose," she said, flipping through Milo Roberts's diary and scanning the words he had written about how much he loved her. She clucked her tongue and then tossed the diary aside. "He was a fool," she said.

"Why's that? For thinking highly of you?" Slocum asked.

Her brown eyes boldly fixed on his green ones.

"No, for not telling me to my face." She reached out and lightly touched his shoulder. Slocum winced. He couldn't help it. The pain was making him dizzy again.

"Sorry," Slocum said. He smoothed the cloth of the sling where his left arm still hung like a dead stump. "I need to find a place to recuperate."

"I can see that," Meg said, studying him closely. She grinned even more broadly and reached out to put her fingers on his cheek. "I've got plenty of room. That suit you, John?"

"That suits me just fine, Meg."

He wondered if he would share Milo Roberts's reticence about this fine woman, who was so honest and upfront and just what he needed to recuperate after being around the Porges family so long.

He didn't think so.

JAKE LOGAN
TODAY'S HOTTEST ACTION WESTERN!